"You were intense [

"Too intense?"

"Perfect," she said, wrapping her arms around his neck to pull him closer. She needed to get him naked, and fast. Her body remembered the warmth of his skin on hers and ached to feel it again. "I want you to be with me the way you want to be with me. Don't hold back. I can take it."

"You took it last night pretty well."

"Only pretty well?"

"Very well," he said, nuzzling his lips to her neck. "You want to take it again?"

"And again and again and again..."

Chris kissed her mouth and she ran her hands down his back. She slipped her hands under his shirt, desperate to touch him. After all that hard work, his body had grown hot to the touch, and her cool skin bristled with pleasure as his heat suffused her.

She wanted more, more, more of him and she couldn't get it fast enough.

Dear Reader,

There are few places in the world more beautiful in autumn than Mount Hood National Forest in Oregon. I should know, because I live here. Shortly after my husband and I moved out to the mountain (technically a volcano), I hired a handful of local contractors to do minor repairs on our new house. They were annoyingly cute and very good at their jobs. I joked to my husband that if I wrote some romance novels about these guys, maybe I could write our home repairs off on our taxes as a book research expense.

Sadly, my accountant didn't go for that idea. But I wrote the books anyway. *Her Halloween Treat* is the first book in the Men at Work trilogy, inspired by the men and women in all our lives who paint our houses, build our decks, landscape our lawns and generally make our neighborhoods nicer places to live. I hope you enjoy the story of Joey, on the rebound after a devastating breakup, and Chris, the sweet and sexy bearded contractor who puts all his handyman skills to use fixing her broken heart.

Enjoy!

With Love from My Secret Volcanic Lair on Mount Hood,

Tiffany Reisz

Tiffany Reisz

Her Halloween Treat

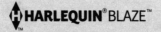

Recycling programs
for this product may
not exist in your area.

ISBN-13: 978-0-373-79916-9

Her Halloween Treat

Copyright © 2016 by Tiffany Reisz

Printed in U.S.A.

Tiffany Reisz is a multi-award-winning and bestselling author. She lives on Mount Hood in Oregon in her secret volcanic lair with her husband, author Andrew Shaffer, two cats and twenty sock monkeys named Gerald. Find her online at tiffanyreisz.com.

Also available from Tiffany Reisz

MIRA Books

The Original Sinners Series

The White Years

*

The Queen
The Virgin
The King
The Saint

The Red Years

*

The Mistress
The Prince
The Angel
The Siren

To get the inside scoop on Harlequin Blaze and its talented writers, visit Facebook.com/BlazeAuthors.

All backlist available in ebook format.

Visit the Author Profile page at Harlequin.com for more titles.

Dedicated to...

Jen LeBlanc—"Don't Stop Believin'," my friend.

1

SHE WANTED TO blame her parents for naming her Jolene. Who did that? Who named their daughter after the most notorious other woman in country music? Once she'd learned who she was named after, Jolene became Joey and there was no going back. And yet just two days ago she'd learned the ugliest truth of her life—she'd been sleeping with a married man.

For two years.

Joey sighed and reached under her sunglasses to wipe a tear from her eyes.

"Jo?"

"Sorry," Joey said.

"You don't have to be sorry, babe." Kira reached over and squeezed her knee. "We're almost to LAX. You need to stop somewhere?"

Joey shook her head. "Keep driving. The sooner I'm out of here, the better. Thanks for getting me."

"I can kill Ben for you, too. I'm willing to kill Ben. In fact, I might do it even if you don't want me to."

When Joey laughed it felt odd, and she realized it was the first time she'd laughed in over thirty-six hours.

"Isn't murder maybe overdoing it?" Joey asked.

"Overdoing it? That piece of shit slept with you in Honolulu and with his wife in LA, and at no point in two years did he tell her about you or you about her? That is what happened, right? I didn't make that up?"

"No, that's right."

"Then it's murder. It's justifiable homicide. And don't argue with me when I'm right. You know I am."

Joey didn't argue. She couldn't because it was all true. For two years Ben had been her boyfriend. They worked together. They played together. They slept together. She believed him when he told her how much he hated living in LA. That he treasured his time with her in Hawaii. He'd move there permanently if he could, but work wouldn't let him. Blah blah blah. Lies, all of it. Lies she'd believed, which is why she routed her flight through LA so she could surprise him. And surprise him she did. She knocked on his door and his wife answered. Quite a surprise for them all.

"So…murder?" Kira asked.

"No murder. Not yet, anyway." She needed to fall out of love with Ben first. Hating him was easy. Not loving him was the hard part.

"Okay. But you just say the word, and I'm there. At the very least you should let me cut his balls off." Kira grinned devilishly at her as she merged onto the I-105 ramp.

Joey swallowed hard, nodded. "Okay," she said. "But just the balls."

Kira dropped her at the terminal and helped her with her bags. Joey slammed the trunk shut and felt better. Slamming things, hitting things—she wanted to destroy all the things. Instead, she just rested her head against Kira's shoulder.

"I wanted to marry him," Joey said.

"I know." Kira roughly patted her back. "I know you did."

"I should have known. I mean, two whole years without him inviting me to LA?"

"I live in LA and I don't even want to be invited to LA. This isn't your fault."

"What do I do?" Joey looked up at Kira. They'd worked together in the Honolulu office of Oahu Air, Oahu's premier business- and first-class airline, before Kira had transferred back to the California office. They'd become fast friends and still were, even with half an ocean between them.

"Look. Here's what you do. You go home to Oregon, you hang out with your family, you have the best time ever at your brother's wedding and you bang the first hot guy you see the second your plane lands."

"What if he's the baggage handler? He might be a little busy."

"Get your bag first. Then bang him."

"I knew I could count on you for good bad advice."

"I'm serious. Find a new guy. No guilt. No shame. No remorse. This isn't about love. This is about you taking care of you. Sexually. It would piss Ben off, right? You jumping into bed with someone else right away?"

"If I burned his house down and threw his dad's signed Gil Hodges home run ball in the ocean, it wouldn't piss him off as much as me sleeping with somebody else right away."

"Then go get it and get it good."

"I don't want to get it. The last thing I can think about right now is dating somebody else."

"Whoa there. Nobody said anything about dating.

This is sex. No strings attached. Speaking to you as a twice-divorced woman, you are not allowed to date somebody new for six months. Sex is fine. Sex is good. Dating'll get you into trouble. Also don't buy a car, a house, a Birkin bag, or go to Vegas with five thousand dollars in your underwear."

"Did you do all of those after your divorce?"

"Everything but the Birkin bag. Those bitches are pricey. So no bags. Unless you get one for me, too. But sex, yes." Kira pointed her well-manicured finger right at Joey's nose. "Have insane, hot, totally meaningless sex until you remember what a goddess you are and you've forgotten Ben's name because you've been too busy screaming some other guy's."

Joey took Kira's finger in her hand and squeezed it.

"You're a good friend. Thank you for enabling my bad behavior."

"It's what friends are for."

The drop-off lane was clogged with cars. As much as Joey hated to be alone, she couldn't put it off any longer.

"Thanks again. I'll text you when I land."

"Do it. And text me when you find a new guy."

Joey grinned. "I will. If I find a new guy."

"You will. I know it. Just remember—it's Oregon. That's hipster and lumberjack territory."

"So?"

Kira pointed at her inner thighs. "Watch out for beard rash downstairs. I speak from experience."

JOEY BOARDED HER FLIGHT—a nonstop, thank God, which meant she'd land in Portland in under two hours. Being alone on a plane, cut off from the world with nothing but her thoughts to keep her company, was not what a woman who discovered she'd been inadvertently in love with a married man for two years needed. With no internet to distract her, all Joey could do was think about the signs she missed. Ben had been the seemingly ideal boyfriend—always attentive, always thoughtful. If he had to miss her birthday one week because he had to be in LA, he'd give her the belated birthday celebration of a lifetime the next week when he came back to Honolulu. Two nights at a five-star hotel. Room service. Wine. A helicopter tour the next day. And sex, so much sex, all night long. But no matter how much she tried to reciprocate, he wouldn't let her. She'd offered to do her part, come visit him, even get a transfer to California. He'd have nothing of it. She was his "sanctuary," he'd said. He couldn't imagine Hawaii without her, he'd said. Someday he'd take over as president of the company and live in Honolulu with her, he'd said. She just had to hold on a few more years, and then they'd be set for life.

Wait a few more years? Yeah, she had to wait a few more years until he had the money or the guts to leave his wife. If that even was his plan. Maybe he'd been stringing her along. She would never forget that moment Saturday morning when she'd hopped a cab from LAX to his house in West LA. She had his address, of course. She'd seen it on his checks, on work forms, on his California driver's license. She'd expected him to be home. And he was home. He was home and so was his wife, Shannon. Shannon answered the door with a confused smile and a "Yes? Can I help you?" Joey, equally confused, said, "I'm looking for my boyfriend. Is Ben home?"

That was the moment Ben stepped into the hallway, his Nikes squeaking slightly on the ocean-blue tile flooring. He was a handsome man, almost six feet tall, dark hair, dark eyes, a devilish grin but with a dimple that made a girl forgive the devil in him.

If she'd had any hope this was all a mistake, it evaporated the second Ben opened his mouth.

"What the hell are you doing here?" Ben had said with unmistakable fury. He'd never looked at her like that before, talked to her like that before. He'd always been happy to see her. If he wasn't happy to see her, it was because that pretty lady holding the door open and looking at him, then looking at her and then looking back at him, wasn't some well-dressed cleaning lady, but his wife. And Ben's wife was having as bad of a day as Ben's girlfriend was.

"Surprise" was the only word Joey could think to say. Shannon had a few other choice words to say and Joey heard them all as she walked to the curb where her cab waited just in case Ben hadn't been home. As the cab pulled away, Joey had turned around to see Ben running toward her. She couldn't read the look on his face—not fury, but not regret, either. She didn't care why he ran after her. Didn't care at all. She was numb with shock and grief. She felt nothing and would never feel anything but nothing again. At least that's what she told herself as she fixed her makeup in a bathroom in the Portland airport. If she never loved again, she'd never hurt again and wouldn't that be lovely?

After doing the best repair job she could on her face, she picked up her luggage and the rental car. It was nice doing normal things, nice to do boring human things. Life went on. Cars still needed renting. Luggage still needed picking up. Brothers still got married. Sisters still went to their weddings. The world didn't end just because a man told a lie. That was good. The world would have ended a long time ago and many times over if it did.

The drive from the airport to her family's old cabin near Lost Lake on Mount Hood was about two hours. Two beautiful hours once she was out on Highway 26 and heading west. She passed over a subtle ridge and what little was left of the city disappeared. There was nothing around for miles but the mountain, a billion trees and low-hanging clouds that brushed the treetops and rolled through the forest like gentle smoke. While Oregon was known for its evergreens, the forests had deciduous trees aplenty and they'd all gone wild with autumn colors—red and orange and lemon yellow. Even in her grief, Joey admired the beauty, took comfort in it. Hawaii was beautiful like nowhere else in the world, but damn, she had missed Oregon's forests. The scent—there was nothing like it. Clean, so clean—pure pine and fir and all so light and airy that if you didn't stop to breathe in deeply enough you'd miss it. But if you did breathe in on a rainy, windy day you might just smell what the world smelled like right after it was born. The trees lay so thick on Mount Hood they looked like an oil painting with the paints piled in heavy layers of emerald and black.

Finally she turned onto the winding gravel road that lead to her parents' old Lost Lake cabin. Her phone vibrated in her pants pocket and she fished it out—carefully.

"Kira, you owe me five hundred dollars if I get caught talking to you," she said when she answered.

"What? Five hundred dollars?"

"Five-hundred-dollar fine in Oregon for talking on your phone while driving."

"Then why did you answer the damn phone?" Kira demanded.

"I'm on my driveway, actually, and the speed limit is five miles per hour. I think I got this."

"Good. Found a guy to bang yet?"

"Do we really have to call it banging? Sounds so… violent."

"Screwing? Fucking? Knocking boots?"

"Knocking boots? How old are you?" Joey asked.

"Just answer the question."

"No, in the four hours since I last saw you I didn't magically meet someone and screw, fuck or knock boots with him in the airport. And I'm probably not going to meet one in the next four hours, either. Or the next four days or the next two weeks. You know Lost Lake is mostly a retirement community, right? Retirees and summer vacation rentals. The only full-timers are the people who work at the lake and that's, like…twenty people."

"Twenty? About half of them must be guys. I like those odds."

"I don't."

"Why are you staying way out there, anyway? You can go find a hot man bun in Portland."

"The cabin is free. Mom and Dad gave it to Dillon as a wedding gift."

"Nice gift. What do you get when you get married?" Kira asked.

"They're paying for my wedding and honeymoon. Better deal than the cabin."

"That bad?"

"It was almost a dump when I was a kid," Joey said. "Now it's *just* a dump. Nobody's stayed in it in ten years as far as I know. Dillon swears up and down he got someone to clean it up a little, but he's been up to his eyeballs in wedding planning. As long as I don't have to bunk with a raccoon, it'll be fine. I can rough it."

"Better you than me. Just let me know if you need me to come up and stay with you a couple days. I mean—in a hotel, but near you. I have some vacation days banked in case of emergency. Best friend accidentally fucking a married dude for two years qualifies."

"It's okay. But I appreciate it. I should go. I'm at the house."

"How bad is it? Bad? Are there snakes? Don't tell me."

Joey could hear the wincing in Kira's voice. Staying at a four-star hotel was her version of "roughing it." She parked the car in the gravel parking spot and was pleased to see the exterior of the house was in better shape than she remembered it. Much better.

"Looks good actually. They painted it. It used to be this dull green but now it's gray. Very pretty," Joey said as she got out of the car. "Looks like cedar shingles."

"Fancy."

"And the landscaping is nice, too. Someone cleaned up the yard."

The trees and shrubs looked well-trimmed. The old broken stone path leading from the driveway to the front porch had been repaired. Every stone fit neatly and perfectly into its place. She didn't trip like she used to when she was a kid and not paying attention to the treacherous walk.

"And somebody decorated?" she said, clinging to

Kira on the phone. "I don't think this is the same house. Did I go to the wrong house?"

"Did you?"

"No. It's 1414 Cottonwood Way. This is it. There are carved jack-o'-lanterns on the porch. Really good ones." She admired the mysterious carver's handiwork. One scary face. One grinning face. One face that looked eerily like Eddie Vedder if Eddie Vedder were a jack-o'-lantern.

"Wait a minute…" Joey said.

"What?"

"Something is definitely up." Joey lifted the welcome mat—when did they get a welcome mat?—pulled out the key and opened the front door. She'd been expecting a bare-bones cabin. That's how she remembered it, anyway. Her parents bought the place for a song when she was seven years old and never remodeled it, never refurbished it, but they'd certainly gotten their money's worth out of it those long summers they'd spent here. Structurally, it was sound, watertight and well-insulated. But inside it had always housed yard sale furniture, squeaky metal cots and second-hand bunk beds, unpainted walls and a kitchen that made cooking on a campfire look inviting. But now…

"Wow," Joey breathed. "Dillon must have decided to live here with Oscar after the wedding. Although I could have sworn he said Oscar hated nature."

"Maybe he changed his mind? Love will do that to a guy."

"Maybe…but still. This is like *Architectural Digest* gorgeous now. I don't even want to think about how much this cost." She turned in a slow circle in the living room. All the yard sale furniture was gone and in its place she found a distressed cedar coffee table, a large rustic leather sofa, a vintage oak rocking chair with what looked like a hand-knitted burgundy throw blanket tossed over the back. Someone had polished the floors to a high shine. The small woodstove had been replaced by a large stone fireplace with a rough wood mantel. And the kitchen had new tile on the floor, a fresh coat of rustic red paint, new rugs, new appliances—nothing but the basics but they were all high quality. Under the sink she found a recycling bin with the toaster box in it. It was that new.

"I wonder if they're fixing it up to sell it."

"House flipping?"

"Maybe. Still, nice of them to spruce it up before I came to stay in it."

"Very nice."

"Probably their way of making up for the fact that my lovely brother scheduled his wedding on my birthday."

"Your fault for being born on Halloween. Perfect day for a Portland wedding."

"Dillon and Oscar do love dressing up. It's an '80s movie theme. I have to pick a costume. Maybe I'll go as Carrie."

"Carrie?"

"You know—the girl with the blood and the prom and all the murdering—that Carrie."

"You're going as a mass murderer to your brother's wedding?"

"It fits my mood."

Except her mood was lifting a little. How could it not in this cabin, this beautiful cozy cabin in the woods? All the place was missing was a man to share it with. She and Ben would have had great sex in this cabin in the woods. They'd be in bed already. But that wasn't going to happen. Not now or ever. Ben had committed an unforgivable sin. He'd lied to his wife. He'd lied to her. He'd betrayed her trust on the deepest level possible, and she would never take him back no matter how lonely she felt without him. And she did feel so terribly alone.

"This is a sex cabin, Kira."

"Sounds like it."

"I'm in a sex cabin, and I can't have sex. This is depressing."

"You can have sex. Go find someone to have sex with. Right now."

"I'm in the middle of the woods. The next cabin is half a mile west."

"Then start walking. Bigfoot's probably out there. He's probably well-hung."

"And hairy."

"I warned you about the beard rash thing."

The floor creaked with the sound of footsteps.

But not hers. Joey hadn't moved.

"Shit," she whispered into the phone.

"What?" Kira whispered back, unnecessarily.

Joey looked up at the ceiling.

"Someone's here. Stay on the line with me."

"Yeah, of course. Are you sure?"

"I heard footsteps upstairs."

"Then get the fuck out of the house. This isn't a horror movie. Do not investigate."

"Right. Going. Right now."

Joey started backing up toward the door, her heart racing. The footsteps continued across the floor above her head. They were fast and purposeful footsteps, not at all tentative but also not threatening. They were heavy, too, like whoever was walking wore either work boots or cowboy boots. She hadn't heard that sound in a long time. Even the VPs at her Oahu Air office often came to work in sandals or flip-flops—one of the perks of working one hundred yards or so from the ocean.

"Jo? You there?" Kira whispered again.

"I'm here. Hello?"

"Yes, I'm still here."

"Not you. I was talking to whoever's up there. I think he's working here."

"Hey there," came a voice from the top of the stairs. A male voice. A deep yet friendly voice. "Joey Silvia?"

"That's me. And you are?"

"It's Chris. I'm almost done up here with the ceiling fan," the man called down to her.

"Has he murdered you yet?" Kira asked.

"Not yet. He says his name is Chris, and he's doing something with the ceiling fan."

"Is he hot?"

"Am I supposed to run screaming from him or have sex with him?" Joey whispered.

"Depends on if he's hot or not. Go look."

"You just told me to leave," Joey half whispered, half yelled.

"You can leave, but find out if he's hot first."

"Okay… I'm going up. If my phone dies and/or you hear the sound of me screaming, hang up and call the cops."

"What if he's not murdering you, but you're screaming because it's such good sex? Do I still call the cops?"

"I'm not a screamer."

"If he's the right guy you will be."

"I'm going to go up and see what he's doing." She glanced out the kitchen window and saw a large green Ford pickup parked behind the house with the words Lost Lake Painting and Contracting on the side in black-and-gold letters. Okay, not an ax murderer, then. Just the guy she should probably thank for doing such a good job on the house.

"I'll stay on the line," Kira said. "If you think he's going to murder you, say, um, 'I'm on the phone with my best friend, Kira. She's a cop. And she's sleeping with a cop. No, two cops. Cop threesome.'"

"I'm just supposed to work that into a casual conversation with a possible murderer?"

"And if he's sexy and you want to bang him, just say, 'Nice weather we're having, isn't it?'"

"It's the Pacific Northwest. In October. It's forty-eight degrees out and raining."

"Just say it!"

"You are the worst friend ever."

"You're welcome. Now go check him out. Try not to get murdered."

Joey crept up the stairs and found they no longer squeaked like they used to. The rotting middle board they had to step over was gone. Someone had replaced the old stairs with beautiful reclaimed pine from the looks of it.

"You still there?" Joey said as she made it to the top of the stairs.

"I'm still here," Kira replied. "You're not dead yet?"

"Not dead. Yet."

The upstairs of the cabin consisted of two small bedrooms with a full bath between them. And whatever magic had been done on the downstairs had wended its way upstairs, too. New bathroom fixtures of brushed copper. The grimy tub had been replaced with a new and huge bathtub inlaid with stone tile. Somehow this Lost Lake contractor had managed to make the house look both old and authentic and yet brand-new at the same time.

"Hello?" she called out.

"I'm in the master," the male voice answered.

"I heard his voice," Kira said over the line. "Good voice. Calm and manly. He's probably comfortable hugging his guy friends and telling his dad he loves him."

"You got that much from four words?" Joey asked.

"I'm very intuitive."

Joey shook her head and walked down the narrow hallway to a partly open door. This had to be the master bedroom, not that she'd ever thought of it like that. *Master bedroom* sounded imposing, impressive. The "master" bedroom she remembered had a tablecloth for a curtain and a mattress propped up on a sheet of plywood and cinder blocks where her parents slept.

"I'm going in," Joey said under her breath, her phone still plastered to her ear.

She eased the door open…stepped inside…looked up…

There on a step stool stood a man, a much younger man than she expected. All contractors were forty and up in her mind but this guy looked no more than late twenties maybe. He had dirty-blond hair cut neat and a close-trimmed nearly blond beard. He was looking up, concentrating on the wiring above his head. He wore jeans, neither tight nor baggy but perfectly fitted, and a red-and-navy flannel shirt, sleeves rolled up to his elbows, with a fitted white T-shirt underneath.

"Hey, Joey," he said with a grin. "Good to see you again. How's Hawaii been treating you?"

He turned his head her way and grinned at her. She knew that grin.

"Chris?" This Chris was *that* Chris?

"Chris? Who's Chris? You know this guy?" Kira rasped in her ear.

She knew this guy. It was Chris, wasn't it?

Oh, my God, it *was* Chris.

Chris… Chris Steffensen. Dillon's high school best friend. The skinny, scrawny, long-haired, baggy-pants-wearing, Nirvana wannabe even a decade after Nirvana was an appropriate thing to be obsessed with at their high school… This was *that* Chris? That Chris she wouldn't have trusted to screw in a lightbulb, and now he was wiring up a ceiling fan? And seemed to be doing a very good job of it.

"Did you…did you fix up this whole house?" she asked, rudely ignoring his question about Hawaii.

"Oh, yeah. I'm doing some work for Dillon and Oscar these days. Long story. You like what we did with the place?"

He grinned again, a boyish eager grin. She couldn't see anything else in the world because that bright white toothy smile took over his face and her entire field of vision. Damn, he was pretty. When did he get so pretty? And he was taller than she remembered. He must have had a bit of a post-high-school growth spurt. Taller and broader. Those shoulders of his…well, there was only one thing to say about that.

Joey hoped Kira was still listening.

"Nice weather we're having, isn't it?"

2

CHRIS STARED AT HER, brow furrowed.

"Joking," she said. "I know it's bad weather."

"It's Oregon weather. Should we awkwardly hug now?"

"God, yes."

"I'm going to hang up," Kira said, laughing into Joey's ear. Joey ended the call and stuffed her phone into her jacket pocket.

"Did you…just hang up on somebody?" Chris asked, his eyebrow slightly arched. When did he learn how to do that?

"Yes. No. She hung up on me first. It's okay. We're friends. We do that a lot. Hug now?"

He jumped lightly down from his stool, and Joey stepped into his arms. He'd said "awkward" and it was but also it wasn't. First of all, he felt good—warm and solid and strong. And second, he smelled good, like sweat and cedar. Finally, it was just Chris, after all, even if it had been nearly ten years since she'd seen him.

"God, it's good to see you again," he said softly, like he meant it. It was the absolute opposite of Ben's *What the hell are you doing here?*

"Yeah, you, too." She stepped back out of his arms before making a fool of herself by bursting into tears.

"You're a day early. Dillon said you wouldn't be here until tomorrow."

"I changed my flight. Is that a problem?"

"Not a problem at all. I just meant to be out of here by then. But I'm almost done. The master was the last thing. Ceiling fan, then paint."

"No hurry. Stay as long as you need to. All night even." She winced. Why did she say that? "So…how are you?"

"Fine." He sounded slightly suspicious. She didn't blame him. She was acting slightly odd. Finding out you'd been dating a married man could do that to a girl. "You? How's Hawaii?"

"Lovely. Lots of volcanoes."

"You're on a volcano right now."

"Hawaii and Oregon have a lot in common. Volcanoes and rain. And…that's it."

"They're practically twins. You look great, by the way," Chris said.

"I'm wet."

Chris's eyebrow went up another notch.

"Wet from the rain," she said hastily.

"Right. The rain. Hawaii's been good to you."

It was sweet that he said that, but she looked like hell and she knew it. She'd dressed in the classic Oregon uniform of Columbia jacket (red), jeans (blue), rain boots (a nondescript army green) and no umbrella. Umbrellas were for tourists, which meant her dark hair was plastered to her forehead. And she'd cried a little in the car and given herself raccoon eyes. She had naturally warm brown skin, which she'd inherited from her Mexican-

American father, and a Hawaiian tan on top of it, so at least she wouldn't appear as washed out as she felt. If she'd known Chris would be here looking as good as he did, she would have made more of an effort.

"You look fantastic. I barely recognized you with the short hair and beard. When did that happen?"

"Short hair? Um, eight years ago? The real world made me do it. The beard? Last November. Bad breakup. She dumped me for a Trail Blazer. I stopped shaving. Everyone told me I looked better with the beard so I kept it. I trimmed it, though. I had a little ZZ Top thing going on."

"A Trail Blazer? Like one of the basketball players or the cars? Because if she dumped you for a car, that's weird."

"The basketball players. Apparently she had a thing for tall guys."

"You're tall. You're huge."

That eyebrow went up one more notch.

"I keep saying sexual things without meaning to," she said. "Sorry. I'm running on very little sleep. I can't be held responsible for what my mouth does."

The eyebrow was as high as it could go.

"I did it again, didn't I?" she asked.

"It's okay, Jo." He furrowed his brow. "Do you still go by Jo? Joey? I don't want to call you that if you don't. Are you Jolene now?"

"Definitely not Jolene. Everyone still calls me Jo or Joey. They better since it's all I answer to."

"Joey, it is. I'm almost done here, and then I'll get out of your hair."

"You aren't in my hair at all. The cabin looks amazing. I can't believe you did all this."

"Not all of it. I had to subcontract the exterior. I can do cedar siding but it takes forever."

"But the rest of it? The floors, the kitchen, the paint… the pumpkins?"

"Some kids were selling pumpkins at a stand by the road. I'm a sucker."

"Were you always good at painting and flooring and advanced pumpkin carving and you just kept it a secret?"

He shrugged. "I learned a lot of it from Dad. Except the pumpkin carving. That's self-taught."

"You go to school for this?"

He nodded. "Yeah, trade school. Then I apprenticed for a few years. Anybody can learn to do this stuff. Just takes time."

"Mount Hood must keep you busy. Half the cabins around here were falling down when we were kids."

"Yeah, tell me about it. I had to turn down four other jobs to do this one for Dillon."

"You could have told him no."

"Nah." He grinned again. "He said you'd be staying here for the wedding. I couldn't let my high school crush crash in a dump, could I? If the ceiling caved in on you, I'd never forgive myself."

Joey laughed, rolled her eyes.

"So *now* you finally admit it."

"Only took me ten years. But don't worry. I'm totally over you." He waved his hand, signing a "done" motion. She might have believed him but for the twinkle of mirth in his eyes.

"You never told me…were you the one who put the roses in my locker on Valentine's Day?"

"Maybe…"

"Did you pick my lock?"

"No. Dillon did."

"Oh, that asshole." She shook her head in exasperation. "I told him I was going nuts trying to figure out who did it, and he played dumb. He's so good at playing dumb I believed him. Or maybe I thought he was just dumb."

"He didn't want to out me. He'd been through that himself."

"Yeah, that was a rough year," Joey said, remembering the year when the rumors about Dillon being gay got started. He'd trusted the wrong friend with the secret and in a week the entire school knew. She and Chris had taken shifts with Dillon, walking with him to and from class, to and from home. As long as there were witnesses around, they were pretty sure nobody would jump Dillon and beat the shit out of him. They'd had a few close calls. Chris had bloodied more than one nose protecting Dillon. "I'm so glad he had you back then."

At least this time he didn't raise his eyebrow at her, but she could tell he wanted to.

"You know what I mean," she said. "Not *had* you. Unless he did. Which is fine. I kind of wondered what you two were up to in the garage."

"Smoking weed."

"That's not sexy at all."

"Sorry to disappoint you with my straightness. I promise, I was born this way."

"It's quite disappointing. I already had yours and Dillon's wedding planned before my own."

"That's far-thinking of you. That wasn't even legal until last year here."

"I was a dreamer. And I thought you'd both look so cute in bow ties."

"I've never been happier to be not marrying Dillon than I am right now."

"No respect for the bow tie. It's a classic. James Bond wore a bow tie. Brando wore a bow tie."

"Pee-wee Herman wore a bow tie."

"Yes, Pee-wee." She pointed at his chest. "That's who you should be for the wedding. You are going, aren't you?"

"I'm going," he said. "I wasn't really planning on wearing a costume, though."

"You have to. It's on the invitation. And *Pee-wee's Big Adventure* was an '80s movie."

"How about a costume that doesn't involve bow ties? Maybe something more along the lines of John Mc-Clane. *Die Hard*, maybe? Easy costume."

"So you'll just wear gray slacks and a dirty nasty white T-shirt to the wedding?" She feigned disgust but the thought of Chris in a sweaty sleeveless undershirt was quite…nice. Nice as the weather they weren't having right now.

"And bloody feet. Don't forget that part. Who are you going as?"

"I was thinking Carrie. Bloody prom dress to match your bloody feet."

"*Carrie* came out in the '70s."

"You sure?"

"I've seen every Stephen King movie at least five times."

"Five times? What is wrong with you?"

"Don't ask," he said.

"Got any other ideas?"

"Got a metal bikini? You can be Princess Leia in *Return of the Jedi*."

"It's a little chilly for that, don't you think?"

"There goes that fantasy." He smiled again. She blushed. Oh, my God, they were flirting. She was flirting. He was flirting. Flirting was happening. Did Kira make this happen? Or was it Dillon? Was he trying to put her and Chris alone in the house together? Very possible. Dillon never liked Ben. And she knew a setup when she saw one.

"So…who are Oscar and Dillon going as?" Chris asked.

"They won't tell anybody. It's a big gay secret, Dillon said."

"He called it a 'big gay secret'?" Chris asked.

"You know my brother."

"Intimately," he said. "Wait. Never mind."

"Any guesses?" Joey asked.

"Kirk and Spock from one of those '80s *Star Trek* movies. They're both nerds. It could work. Walking, talking fan fiction."

"My money's on Bill and Ted," Joey said.

"Whoa."

"Exactly."

"You know who you should go as…" Chris pointed his screwdriver at her and it was neither threatening nor sexual. Especially when he flipped it casually and stuck it in his back pocket like a kid gunslinger holstering a toy pistol.

"Who?"

"Since the guys hijacked your birthday for their wedding…you should go as what's-her-name from that movie."

"That doesn't help me."

"Girl. Redhead. Birthday cake." He snapped his fingers repeatedly. "You know, Molly Something."

"*Sixteen Candles*?"

"That's it. Didn't her sister get married on her birthday?" Chris asked.

"Day after but close enough. Oh, my God, that's a great idea. Dillon will think it's hilarious. He loves that movie. I'll go as Sam. All I have to do is get a red wig and a floofy bridesmaid dress. Or some kind of Laura Ashley nightmare to wear and a hat. Will you come with me?"

"As who? Don't say Dong."

"No, you can put on a pink button-down shirt and be Farmer Ted. Just pop your collar."

"Will you let me walk around with your underwear in my pocket like he did?"

"You remembered my birthday. You can walk around with my underwear in your teeth if you want."

Chris's eyes widened just slightly.

"This conversation got weird fast," she said.

"I've never had anyone offer to let me hold their underwear in my mouth at a wedding."

"Well, it is Dillon's wedding."

"Fair point."

She rocked back on her heels. "I'm just gonna get my stuff out of the car. Or maybe I should wait since the bedroom's not done yet."

"The other bedroom is all set up. You can put your stuff in there."

"Our old bedroom? You fixed it up?"

"I did. Go check it out. Turned out pretty nice."

He wore an expression on his face that made her a

teeny tiny bit suspicious. She walked out of the master bedroom and down the hall into the second bedroom. She'd always liked that room better. Better view of the forest and she could even catch the occasional glimpse of Mount Hood's snowy peak on clear days.

She opened the door and her jaw dropped. Chris had outdone himself. The plaster that covered the walls had been removed, leaving the rough wood boards exposed. They gleamed a golden hue in the warm lamplight. A hand-woven blue-and-gray rug covered most of the hardwood floor. A large bed sat in the center of the room. The headboard and footboard were all dark wood, roughly carved but sanded smooth, stained and polished. Piled high on the bed were pillows and blankets. The downstairs woodstove had been brought up to the guest room and a hole cut into the wall to vent it properly. Framed photographs of Mount Hood and the surrounding forest in all seasons lined the walls. It was everything rustic and luxurious and lovely all in one. She could be very happy in this room and in this house. Or, at least, not as miserable as she thought she'd be. Even the frames on the photographs were beautiful distressed wood. A small thing but she admired it, was grateful for it.

"You're good," she said as Chris came to stand behind her.

"So I've been told. But don't be too impressed. A friend of mine makes those frames, not me. But I did make the bed."

"You do excellent hospital corners."

He chuckled softly. "No, I mean, I made the bed."

"You...carved the bed?"

"There's all these trees around here. Might as well put them to use."

"You literally made the bed?"

"I literally made the bed. Impressed?"

"I am. Are you trying to impress me?"

"I don't know. It is working?"

"It's sort of working." It was definitely working. "So…you want to get a drink later? My treat."

Kira would be so proud of her, asking Chris out for a drink two days after being dumped.

"You betcha."

She was officially back in Oregon. *You betcha?* When was the last time she heard that?

"But I have to finish up the master first."

"Can I help?"

"You want to help?"

"I wouldn't have offered if I didn't. What are we doing?"

"Painting. I finished painting the ceiling. Gotta paint the walls now. It's all taped off already."

"I can paint. I'm good with the trim."

"You start the trim, I'll roll the walls. But you'll need to take those clothes off."

"Chris, we just, I mean—"

"You'll get paint on your clothes, Jo."

"Right. Paint. I'll…just get my stuff out of the car and change clothes real quick."

"Take your time. I'll finish wiring the ceiling fan."

"Did you make the ceiling fan, too?"

"No. But I did put on the stairs and the stair rail. It's all pine."

"You're really good with wood."

"You did that one on purpose, didn't you?" he asked.

"Let's pretend I did."

Chris didn't laugh at her but she caught him smiling as he left her alone in her new room. Well, not *her* room but the room that would be hers while home for the wedding. She hadn't taken a vacation in a couple years. After everything that had happened with Ben she was tempted to take it all at once and not go back to work until after Thanksgiving. In fact, she was sorely tempted not to go back to work ever. Not there, anyway. Not if she had to face Ben.

Except she'd promised Kira she wouldn't make any major life changes for six months. It was good advice, very wise. She had to go back to work, didn't she? Of course she did. She was in the right and Ben was in the wrong. She wasn't about to let him win by quitting and slinking away with her tail between her legs.

No. Stop. Joey refused to think about Ben or work or anything else as she hauled her suitcase and overnight bag up the reclaimed pine wood stairs and into the bedroom. Funny—she'd been looking forward to a quiet night alone in the cabin before facing her brother and parents and giving them the news about her and Ben. She wanted the one night to pull herself together, to figure out a story to tell her family about why she broke up with Ben that wouldn't make her look like the worst person on earth and/or the stupidest person on earth. But hanging out with Chris and working on the house seemed like a far better way to get her head together than sitting alone in an empty cabin and ruminating on every clue she'd missed, every blind eye she'd turned. Better to work, do something, distract herself, stay busy. Painting the master bedroom with Chris actually sounded sort of fun.

She pulled on an old long-sleeved T-shirt that she slept in and tied a red bandana around her hair. When she went into the master bedroom she found Chris had finished up with the ceiling fan and was pouring a warm brown paint, the color of milk chocolate, into a large plastic tub. He was whistling.

"Is that 'All Apologies'?" she asked as she selected a two-inch paintbrush from his kit on the floor.

"It is."

"You're whistling Nirvana while you work. You know most people whistle happy tunes."

"So 'Heart-Shaped Box,' then?"

She pointed her paintbrush at him. "You've changed completely, but you haven't changed at all."

"I could say the same to you," he said, glancing at her out of the corner of his eyes. She was ninety percent sure he'd just checked her out. Good. She'd been checking him out since she walked in the door.

He handed her a small roller tray filled with paint. She dipped her brush in the tray, soaked it with paint and coated the wall by the doorframe with a smooth line of warm mocha.

"Wait, not that wall," Chris said, his voice full of pure panic.

Joey gasped and spun around "What? Sorry. Did I—"

He grinned. Broadly.

"Oh, you asshole," she said. She brandished her paintbrush in his direction and he ducked.

"I'm not sorry but I want to be sorry."

"I'm going to paint now, and if you scare me like that again, I'll paint your flannel."

"But this is my dress flannel. I wore it to my father's funeral."

"Please tell me you didn't wear a flannel shirt to your dad's funeral. Please."

"I didn't. But only because Dad's still alive."

She sighed, shook her head and got back to painting while Chris returned to his whistling and rolling. He was the same Chris even if this Chris had short hair, a perfect beard and clothes that actually fit his body. His distractingly good body. She made herself focus as she painted. It was nice transforming the dingy beige walls a cozy chocolate color. It was the perfect color for this room. A forest color. A homey color.

"You picked the color?" she asked.

"I did, yeah."

"I love it. I wouldn't have thought a color so dark would look good in here but it does."

"Dark warm colors work best in low-light rooms."

"Did you learn that in trade school?"

"Pinterest."

She stared at him.

"What?" he said. "It's my job."

They returned to their painting. Chris had a Pinterest account. Now that was adorable. He was adorable. If he got any more adorable, she would be forced to adore him.

Joey wished Kira hadn't told her to sleep with the very first guy she could find as part of her recovery strategy. Now she couldn't stop thinking about Chris like that. She wanted to think it was because she was starting to get over the shock of her breakup, but she was afraid she was flirting with Chris just because her best friend told her to, and because she wanted to soothe her bruised heart and ego with the balm of male attention.

Chris wiped sweat off his forehead and peeled out of his flannel shirt. His basic white T-shirt showed off his sinewy forearms and strong muscular biceps to marvelous effect.

Okay, so she was flirting with him because she wanted to and for no other reason. Thanks to those sexy arms of his, her conscience was now officially clear.

"You know what would look good in here? White bed linens," she said. "That would make a nice contrast with the dark brown paint. Like a hotel bed."

"Good idea. That would look hot. I mean, nice."

It would look hot. This room with this paint and that big bed with fresh white Egyptian cotton sheets? She was glad he was thinking what she was thinking.

"I'll pick some up tomorrow," she said.

"I'll do it. I still have Dillon's credit card."

"We could both go tonight. I can help you pick stuff out," she said. It was still early evening. They could make it to Portland or Hood River if they hurried.

"We could get our drink after," Chris said. "Maybe dinner, too?"

Had Chris just asked her out on a date? A real date or a "we knew each other in high school and are morally obligated to catch up with each other" date? She'd assume it was the latter and hope it was the former.

"Dinner sounds great," she said. "Painting made me hungry."

"Me, too. But we did good. Good team." He held out his fist and she bumped it. The room did look pretty amazing.

"It was fun. I needed to get my mind off stuff. This helped."

"What stuff?"

"I don't remember," she said. "That's how well it worked."

"Glad I could help by putting you to work. If you need more distraction, you could clean the gutters."

"You know what? I'm good. But thanks for the offer."

"Dinner now?" he asked.

"Yes, please."

Chris turned on the ceiling fan to help dry the paint more quickly. Joey went to the guest room—her room apparently for the next couple of weeks—to figure out what to wear for their date. Not a date. Not really. Well, sort of a date. She had two missed texts from Kira.

Text message one read, Have you banged him yet?

Text message two read, How about now?

Joey wrote back, No, we haven't banged yet. He's an old friend from high school. We are going out to dinner so stop texting me. If/when there is banging, you will be the first to know.

Then she sent a quick text to Dillon letting him know she made it to the cabin a day early and she'd see him tomorrow unless he was dying to see her tonight, which she knew he wasn't because she still had a feeling he'd planted Chris here in the cabin for nefarious reasons. Seemed like something Dillon would do.

She cleaned up for dinner as quickly as she could. Chris had seen to everything in the house, every little detail. He'd even installed a rain showerhead and put new soft cotton towels in the bathroom linen closet. It was like staying in a hotel, a hotel that came with its own sexy contractor/concierge, which made this the best hotel she'd ever stayed in.

While drying her hair she realized she was smiling. That was good, right? She'd cried all Saturday night on Kira's couch at her place in LA. Smiling was a huge improvement over gut-wrenching sobbing. She felt more human back in Oregon, back on the mountain and near the lake where she'd spent so much of her childhood. If she wanted to go to the lake she could walk there blindfolded—out the back door and down the cut stone path to the edge of the forest. Then five hundred and sixty-eight steps on the dirt path. She knew the exact number because she'd counted as a kid because kids did weird obsessive stuff like count their steps. It was also one thousand one hundred and thirty-seven steps to the main road and nine hundred ninety-one steps to where she and Chris and Dillon had set up their campfires in high school.

It had always been the three of them back then—her and Dillon and Chris. Dillon wasn't the sort of brother to resent his sister's company. He'd needed her, even wanted her, around. Part of it was fear. At age fourteen he'd confessed to her he was ninety-nine percent sure he was gay, and she'd kept his secret for him until he'd worked up the courage to tell their parents. He'd told Chris shortly thereafter, and she and Chris had been first his secret keepers and then his protectors when the secret got out. At the time it hadn't seemed strange that Chris had guarded Dillon's back after her brother got outed at their mostly rural high school. They'd been friends forever. Of course Chris watched out for Dillon because Dillon would have done the same for Chris. But only now, after so many stories in the news about kids and bullies and suicide and school shootings and all that, did it occur to her that Chris had put his life on the line by protecting Dillon. Dillon's life was on the line every single day just for being Dillon, but Chris had been right there with him, throwing punches when needed, and sadly, those punches had been needed.

Thinking back she was so grateful both Dillon and Chris survived those two ugly terrifying years of high school with their bodies and spirits intact. Still, she had to wonder if her constant worrying for her big brother was the reason she never got around to noticing how hot his best friend was?

By the time she finished blow-drying her long, dark hair and dressing in clean jeans, her knee-high leather boots and a red sweater, Chris had finished up in the master.

"Your car or my truck?" he asked as he pulled on his jacket. "Or should we go separately?"

She paused before answering. If they went together in the same vehicle, that meant they'd both have to come back to the cabin tonight. If they drove separately, Joey could come home alone and Chris could return to his place, wherever that was. Driving separately made sense. Driving together made it a date. Chris had left it up to her, like a gentleman. She liked that.

"Your truck," she said. "The only small cars the rental place had left were Miatas. I don't trust rear-wheel drives in Oregon rain."

"I'll drive, then. Truck's a little messy, fair warning."

"I can handle it." She pulled up her jacket hood and opened the front door where she promptly received a slap of frigid sleet right in her face.

She stepped back inside the house and closed the door. She wiped the sleet off her face and looked at Chris.

"Nice weather we're having," he said. "Isn't it?"

3

THEY ATE IN, which was fine. More than fine as Chris had filled the fridge per Dillon's request with all the basics. She threw together a salad while Chris cooked chicken on the George Foreman grill. It wasn't haute cuisine but it tasted a lot better than that mouthful of icy rain and sleet had earlier. While they ate she flipped through her pictures on her phone and showed Chris photos of the beach and her last whale-watching excursion. None of the pictures in her phone were of her and Ben together. He was camera shy, he'd told her. Another red flag she ignored.

Chris took out his phone then and showed her before, during and after pictures of the cabin as he'd cleaned it up and remodeled it. She couldn't believe how thoroughly he'd transformed it.

"This place used to be such a dump," she said. "Remember?"

"It was a nice dump, though," he said. "Lots of good memories here. It was fun working on the place. It needed help."

"How much is all this costing Dillon?" she asked,

waving her fork around the newly remodeled cabin. Now that Chris had fixed the place up so beautifully, she was half-tempted to see if Dillon would sell it to her. Although with all the renovations, it was probably out of her price range.

"Not as much as it should. I gave him a discount on the labor. The interior work was about five. The exterior another five."

"That's not much for this kind of makeover."

"You can swing a lot of bargains if you know what you're doing."

"And you definitely know what you're doing."

"I do now." He took a bite of his salad and it appeared he was trying to cover up a smile. Of what? Pride? Pleasure in her compliment? Because this felt like a date?

"Is Dillon selling the place?"

"Did he say something to you about it?"

She shook her head. "No. Just a guess. I know Oscar's not the mountain-life sort of guy. He said he hates nature so much that when someone says being gay is 'unnatural' he takes it as a compliment because nature is so gross and horrible."

Chris laughed. "Oscar's great. You'll like him."

"So are they selling it?"

"Not selling it. They're planning on renting it out. He asked me to fix it up and gave me a ten thousand dollar limit. I used every penny."

"He can afford it," she said. Dillon made mid-six figures at his law firm, and Oscar was several years older and very well-off from his investment banking job. She didn't begrudge Dillon his success, though, not with the hours he put in. She much preferred her forty-hour workweek and her evenings and weekends off to enjoy her life. And she *had* been enjoying it. Until meeting Ben's wife, that is. But tonight…she was kind of enjoying tonight.

"So…can I ask something?" he said.

"You just did."

He glared at her.

"Ask," she said.

"Why'd you come back?"

"My brother's getting married? I would assume that's a good enough reason."

"No, you said you changed your flight to come back early. You had a weird look on your face when you said it."

"Oh. That." She sat back from the bar. They'd eaten at the bar on counter stools instead of the table. Since the bar was small they sat on opposite sides facing each other. It felt more informal that way, more like friends than the strangers they'd become to each other. "I had booked a couple days in LA between Hawaii and here. I had plans with a friend and they sort of fell through. So I came home a day early."

It was technically true. Her boyfriend was also her friend and she'd had plans for them. She'd barely wrapped her mind around the accidental affair she'd been having for the past two years. She wasn't about to drop all that on Chris's lap. The lap could be used for much better purposes.

"You called it home."

"What?" Joey asked.

"You called Oregon home. You said you came home a day early. Do you still think of Oregon as home?"

"Well… I did grow up here. That makes it home."

"Does Hawaii feel like home?"

"No. Not that that's a bad thing. It's been an adventure, but it's never felt permanent. Maybe it will someday. When I go places and people ask where I'm from I still say Oregon, even though I've been living there for years. So yeah, Oregon is home still. And I'm glad I had it to come home to after…you know, my plans didn't work out. I feel better already being back."

"Sorry your trip didn't work out with your friend."

"It's okay. It's for the best, really. Will you excuse me?"

Joey put her napkin down and walked quickly but not too quickly to the downstairs bathroom. She didn't have to go, but she did need to take a few deep breaths to calm herself down. Crying with Kira all night and a few hours painting a bedroom with Chris wasn't going to heal the wound that fast. But she refused to succumb to tears. Ben didn't deserve any more of her tears.

In the kitchen she heard the distinct beeping of her phone. She'd set it to wolf whistle whenever she got a message.

"That's Dillon," she yelled through the door as she dried her hands. "What does he want?"

"He wants to know if I've banged you yet."

"Oh, shit…" Joey buried her face in her hands, took a deep breath and peeked her head out of the bathroom.

"That text wasn't from Dillon," she said.

Chris eyed her with amusement—thank God.

"Not unless you put him under 'Kira' in your contacts list. I didn't know I was supposed to bang you."

"Ugh."

"Ugh?"

"Yes, ugh." She eased back down onto her bar stool, wincing in her extreme embarrassment. "I have to tell you something."

"Before or after I bang you?"

She grimaced. "Cute. Here's the thing." She clasped her hands in front of her.

"How do you feel about spooning? I'm for it myself if I get to be the big spoon."

"Now I remember why I didn't have a crush on you in high school."

He laughed, which was good. Better than getting up and leaving before she could explain herself.

"I told you I had plans with a friend in LA and they didn't work out? Well… I have a boyfriend. Had a boyfriend. At least, I thought he was a boyfriend."

"What was he?"

"A husband."

"He was your husband?"

"No. He wasn't my husband. That's the problem."

Chris started to sit back but then clearly realized he was on a bar stool and leaned forward instead.

"That doesn't sound good."

"No…no, it really isn't good. Ben works at Oahu Air. He's one of the VPs there. Luckily not of my department. He commutes from LA. Couple weeks in Honolulu. Couple weeks in LA. He says he hates LA, and I believed him, but I like LA so I thought I'd visit him there. A surprise. Happy surprise? No. Not happy surprise."

"What happened?"

"I went to his house and rang the bell, and his wife opened the door."

"Fuck."

"My sentiments exactly. Two years. We dated two years. Nobody at work knew he was married. He kept it a secret for whatever reason. Probably so he could date in Hawaii, which he did. We were together two years before I figured out he was married. And I didn't even figure it out. It had to be shoved down my throat." She took a ragged breath. "So…as you can imagine, I'm feeling pretty stupid."

"You shouldn't feel stupid. Sounds like he had his game down pat."

"Nobody at work knew. Not even my friend Kira, who worked with him in the LA office. Kira told me that the best way to get over one guy is to get under another."

"It's a sound theory, really."

"When I got here I was on the phone with her. And I told her you were cute, and she told me to sleep with you. I told her to mind her own business. She's not good at that part. As you saw. Again, sorry. That was awkward."

"You're having a bad week. It's okay."

"You know, Dillon never liked Ben. I thought it was because Dillon's never met him. Ben would never come back to visit home with me. He'd only see me in Honolulu. Dillon must have known something was off. I should have known. That should have been a bright red flag in my face."

"Do you remember what you said to me when Cassie dumped me my senior year? It made me feel a lot better."

"I said something?"

"You said something."

"What did I say?"

"You said, 'Forget it. Wanna go see *Batman Begins* with us?'"

"That's it? That's the big thing I said to you?"

"It wasn't a big thing. It was a little thing. It made me feel normal again, going to see a movie with you and Dillon. It made me remember that life goes on and that's a good thing."

"And it was a good movie."

"Fucking A it was."

"So you think we should watch a Batman movie?"

"No."

"What should we do, then?" she asked.

He put his glass of wine down and moved his plate out of the way.

Then he moved her plate out of the way.

Then he leaned across the bar and kissed her lightly on the lips.

Joey's eyes widened as he pulled back.

"I should have asked if I could do that before I did that," he said.

"You can do that."

"I already did it."

"You can do it again."

Chris leaned in again, kissed her again. By the time that kiss was done, she had her smile back.

"And again," she said.

"Are you sure? This is a little weird." Chris winced. He was even cute wincing and that was cute.

"Weird? Why?"

"Because I wanted to do this ten years ago. And then I didn't think about it for, oh, nine years and six months or so. And now…here I am doing it. High school me is freaking out."

"What about grown-up you?"

"He's freaking out, too. But in a much cooler way. Like, so cool you can't even tell."

"I can tell," she said.

"How?" The corners of his eyes crinkled a little when he smiled.

"Because I'm freaking out and I'm projecting."

"You're prettier than you were in high school, and in high school you were perfect."

"You're prettier than you were in high school, too."

"And?"

"And…"

"I didn't look perfect in high school?"

"You wore a chain wallet."

"So there was a lot of room for improvement."

"You improved. You definitely improved." She leaned forward and kissed him back.

He deepened the kiss subtly and gently, but she felt the change. The first kiss had been tentative and sweet, the second kiss playful and now this third kiss…this third kiss was something else entirely.

Ben didn't have a beard. No facial hair at all. And she was pretty sure she'd never kissed a guy with a real beard, not just a five-o'clock shadow. Very quickly she decided she liked it. The hair tickled her top lip and her chin while he softly kissed her lips, and when the tickling grew to be too much, she opened her mouth to him and he slipped his tongue between her teeth.

This was now officially a real kiss. A really real kiss. A kiss that was going places. She cupped his face, lightly stroking his chin and cheeks with her thumbs as she deepened the kiss. Chris made a soft sound in the back of his throat, a distinct sound, pure pleasure. She wanted to hear it again.

And again…

Joey couldn't believe she was doing this, kissing

Chris. Not because it was Chris so much as it wasn't Ben. Kira told her the quickest way to get over one guy was to get under another, but that was Kira's thing, not hers. Joey never even dated in high school and had one boyfriend in college. She'd never had a one-night stand, never took risks like this, making out—and maybe more—with someone who'd been a virtual stranger all of two hours ago.

Except he wasn't a virtual stranger even if they hadn't seen each other in years. This was Chris Steffensen. He'd driven her and Dillon to school for two straight years of high school. He'd taught her how to shoot a bow and arrow one summer at the lake. He'd walked on her brother's left side while she'd walked on his right between classes Dillon's senior year when the bullying was at its absolute worst and she had actual nightmares her brother would be the next Matthew Shepard. But Dillon had made it through that awful time and gone off to college in New York. Meanwhile Chris had gone to work and she hadn't given him much thought since then.

"I wish we hadn't lost touch after school," she said against his lips.

"Losing touch isn't that bad as long as you, I don't know, start finding touch again."

She smiled into his lips and touched his face once more. "I think I found it."

With the bar in the way they couldn't do anything but kiss. So they had a couple choices—just keep kissing or find somewhere more comfortable.

"You want to go somewhere more comfortable?" Chris asked.

"You read my mind."

Chris pulled away from the kiss and crooked his finger at her.

"Where are we going?" she asked.

"I was thinking the couch. It's a new couch. It needs christening with a good make-out session."

"Or," she said.

"Or?"

Joey would blame Kira for this tomorrow. Tonight she had no one to blame but herself.

"The bed's new. Why don't we go christen it?"

Chris looked at her a moment. "You sure?"

"We can fool around." She almost said "bang" and that was definitely Kira's fault. "Or we can rent *Batman Begins*. But for either of those things, I'm sure it's more comfortable than the couch. We'll see where it goes, all right?"

"All right. Lead the way, then."

She was shaking with nervousness and excitement as she headed up the stairs. They really were very nice stairs.

"You do such good work," she said.

"I hope you're still saying that an hour from now."

"I was talking about the woodwork."

"That's one name for it."

"Chris."

He pushed her gently back against the wall and kissed her deeply again, not too hard but hard enough she wanted more. A strategic kisser, Chris was—he knew how to make her want more.

And more.

And more…

"You gave me my first kiss," she said.

"You remember?"

She nodded breathlessly. "I'd almost forgotten. It was here at the cabin."

"Out back," he corrected. "We had a campfire."

"Mom and Dad went out to dinner and left the three of us here."

"We got in the liquor cabinet and had a couple shots," he said. "That was a bad idea."

"What? Making s'mores while drunk was the most fun I'd ever had."

"You got chocolate all over your lips," he said. "You told me to help you get it off."

"Where was Dillon?"

"He'd wandered off to piss in the woods."

"Oh, that's right. He got lost and it took him an hour to get back."

The memory was hazy. She'd been fourteen, Chris sixteen, Dillon seventeen, if she remembered correctly. Chris had his hair pulled back in a blond ponytail, and he wore board shorts instead of his usual ratty jeans. That night he'd looked almost handsome and she'd been a raging ball of vibrating estrogen capable of orgasming from a hard sneeze and able to fall in and out of love with total strangers all in the span of one day or less. The Jack Daniel's they'd all dipped into had made her head fuzzy and Chris ten times more talkative than usual. He'd told her dirty stories like the one about the three guys who had to share one bed up at Timber Ridge Lodge, and the guy on the right of the bed wakes up the next day and says, "I had a dream somebody gave me a hand job," and the guy on the left of the bed says, "Crazy, I also had a dream somebody gave me a hand job," and the guy in the middle of the bed said, "Weird. I had a dream I was skiing."

That was what it was. He'd told her the skiing/hand job joke and she'd snort-laughed chocolate from her s'more all over her mouth. And she'd told him he had to help her get it off since it was all his fault that she'd laughed while eating and made a massive mess of herself. She'd expected a napkin, a towel, a leaf, something to clean herself off.

Instead, he'd kissed her. Not a kiss, a lick. He licked her lips, and quickly it turned into a real kiss, her first kiss. Before anything else could happen, they heard Dillon tramping back to camp. She'd hated her brother right then and right there. Why couldn't it have been number two instead of number one, Dillon? Until that moment in her young life, she had no idea having a male tongue on and in her mouth could be the single greatest sensation of all the sensations she'd ever sensated. He'd tasted better than a s'more, and if that wasn't the highest compliment a fourteen-year-old girl could give a guy, she didn't know what was.

"I still think about you when I eat s'mores," he said. "Is that weird?"

"I still think about you every time a Nirvana song comes on the radio."

"That's the sexiest thing any woman has every said to me."

He kissed her again before she could laugh and then she didn't want to laugh anymore. All she wanted was to kiss and kiss and kiss some more. He was a wonderful kisser and she was quickly getting used to the soft tickle of his beard on her lips and chin and cheeks. And a small evil part of her was relishing the knowledge, even reveling in it, maybe also wallowing in it, that Ben would blow a brain gasket if he knew what she was doing right now. He'd always had a jealous streak, which she'd found flattering at first and increasingly irritating over the past few months. It had seemed out of place, uncalled for. She'd never given him a reason to be jealous. Now she knew he'd been projecting, covering up for his own guilty conscience. Well, fuck him. He had no say in what she did anymore.

She pulled back from the kiss only to open the bedroom door. Chris flipped the lights on but only long enough to turn on the lamp and then the overhead lights were off again. There was a definite chill in the air so she sat on the edge of the bed patiently while Chris threw a few logs in the woodstove and started a fire. It was a pleasure to watch him work. He had quick and efficient large hands that moved with surety at every task. Door open, logs in, newspapers in, more logs, match lit and then…fire. Warmth infused the room, which might have had something to do with the fire in the stove and might have had something to do with Chris taking his shirt off. Not the T-shirt, not yet. Just the flannel he wore over it, but the sight of his strong bare arms was enough to raise her temperature a degree or two especially since he was taking it off while walking toward the bed.

"You're not supposed to be this sexy," she said as he came to stand in front of her.

"Sorry?"

She put her hands on his hips, slid them under his white T-shirt and felt his hard flat stomach.

"I accept your apology."

"I'll never do it again."

"See that you don't."

"Do you want to take your shirt off?"

"That's not fair. I only have a bra on under my shirt. You had a T-shirt on under yours."

Chris sighed, a put-upon sigh. Then he took his T-shirt off.

"Better?"

She stared at his chest, at his bare shoulders and stomach. This was a man who worked very hard and his body showed it.

"Much, much better."

Chris reached down and gathered the fabric of her sweater in his hands. She raised her arms and let him pull it off. It joined his flannel and T-shirt on the floor. She really hadn't planned on seducing Chris or being seduced by him tonight, but apparently her subconscious had known better because she'd chosen her favorite plum-colored lace bra to wear under her sweater. Did she remember to put on the matching panties? Oh, yes, she had. Chris would probably assume she'd planned this when he saw them. She hadn't, but she didn't care if he thought that.

He bent and kissed her again. Inch by inch, he eased her onto her back with kisses as he crawled onto the bed, his knees on each side of her hips, his arms bracing himself over her. She might be on her back but she refused to lie there passively while he kissed her lips and neck and chest. With her right hand she cupped the back of his neck. With her left hand she went exploring. He was lean, almost thin despite the presence of some impressive muscles, and when she ran her hand down his back, she could feel the outline of his shoulder blades under his warm skin. She lingered a long time on his back, loving the width of it, the length, the strength. And she couldn't think clearly enough to do much else at the moment as Chris was nuzzling her neck with his mouth, and his beard tickled the tender skin under her ear.

"You feel amazing," he whispered. "And you smell amazing."

"What do I smell like?"

"Like you did in high school. Like cookies."

She laughed as he nipped at her neck. "It's in my perfume. It's vanilla-scented. In high school I just used vanilla extract. I couldn't afford perfume."

"You smell good enough to eat. You always did."

"I'm not going to say it. You're not going to make me say it."

The corners of his eyes crinkled with his grin.

"Say it. You know you want to."

"Eat me, then," she said.

"If you behave yourself."

Now it was her turn to raise her eyebrow at him. She didn't even know she could do that.

"If I behave? How am I supposed to behave?"

Chris kissed his way to her ear and whispered into it one word: "Badly."

Joey shivered from his hot breath on her cool flesh.

He lowered himself onto her carefully, his hips flush against hers, his bare chest to her chest. So much warm skin, so much body heat, so much male weight on top of her... When she'd been weeping on Kira's couch, one of her laments had been how much she'd miss having sex. She loved sex, needed it, wanted it when she could get it, wanted it more when she couldn't. How long would it be before she recovered from this breakup and started dating again, started having sex again? Well...a couple days apparently. She would have laughed except she had

Chris's tongue between her teeth, and she wasn't keen on letting it go just yet.

Joey ran her hands up Chris's arms and rubbed his shoulders and biceps, massaging them as they kissed because she quickly discovered that when she did this, Chris made the loveliest soft moaning sound in the back of his throat and he pushed his hips into hers hard enough she could feel the outline of his erection. Those were all wonderful consequences to a wonderful action.

Chris placed his left hand by her hand and held himself up over her long enough to slide her bra straps down her shoulders. He kissed her neck and arms and chest to tease her and it worked. Oh, how it worked. She was ready to beg him to take her bra all the way off when he upped the teasing ante by cupping her right breast in his hand and lightly squeezing it. Even through the silk fabric she could feel his heat and the gentle pressure. She arched into his hand, wanting more. He brought his mouth down and kissed her nipple through her bra. It puckered and hardened, and the sound she made as he licked her through the silk should have embarrassed her, it was so hungry. But she'd given herself permission to be decadent tonight, to indulge in something she usually didn't do—have a one-night stand with an old friend just to make herself feel better. Chris knew this was all it was, so why not? Why not make herself feel good and him feel good and forget Ben existed, at least for tonight?

"You're good at teasing me," she said.

"Am I?" He nuzzled against the valley of her breasts.

"You're going very slow."

"I like to go slow. If I go fast, then it's over with too soon."

"Or you could go fast—twice."

"You're behaving very badly right now."

"You told me to."

"I know." He raised his head and grinned at her, a grin to set her body temperature shooting up another degree or two. "It was a compliment."

He rewarded her for her bad behavior by pushing the cup of her bra down. The cool air of the room on her naked breast sent her shivering with delicious chills. Chris lightly licked the hard tan tip that was turning a darker shade of brown as he gave it more and more attention and more and more blood rushed to her breasts. She tangled her hand in his hair and held his mouth to her nipple. He covered it with his lips and sucked softly and then deeply and then hard enough to make her gasp aloud.

Chris kissed her mouth after she moaned and took her breast in his hand. He pinched her nipple and tugged lightly on it, rolling it between his fingers as he kissed her until she could scarcely breathe and forgot she needed to.

"Remind me to do something after you're done fucking me," she whispered.

"What is that?"

"I need to call Kira and tell her she's a genius."

4

HE LOWERED HIS head again and gave her left breast the same sort of attention, lavishing kisses on it, sucking the nipple, rolling his tongue around it as she lifted her hips again and again against him, unable to stop herself. Her arousal was potent, sharp in its intensity. She felt everything he did to her all over her body. It was nervousness, of course, and the adrenaline rush that came with a brand-new partner after being with only one man in two years. Also, it felt like she was breaking a rule, cheating, cheating on Ben even though she wasn't. They hadn't said they'd broken up, but there was no reason to say a single word to him the second she discovered he was married. Their relationship was null and void in her mind because he'd lied to her, lied to his wife. But if she knew Ben as well as she thought she did, he would apologize, try to get her back. He still considered her his girlfriend, and if he knew she was with another man, he would lose his mind. She almost wanted to call him right now and tell him what she was doing.

And laugh.

"More," she whispered as Chris lightly bit her nipple.

"More what?"

"More of you," she said, sliding her palms down his body from his neck to the small of his back where she lingered awhile. His skin was so soft here, so touchable, so smooth. "More of this." She lifted her pelvis meaningfully into his.

"Are you begging for sex?"

"Not yet. Should I?"

"Worth a try. Maybe it would work."

"No guy has ever made me beg for it before."

"Maybe I know it's worth begging for."

"You're a little cocky, Chris. How did I not know that about you?"

"A little cocky?"

She smiled.

He rose up off her body, knelt over her hips and unzipped his jeans. He lowered them and his black boxer briefs to his thighs. With one hand he stroked himself over her.

"Okay," she said breathlessly. "You're a lot cocky." When he started to raise his jeans up again—more teasing—she reached out and grabbed his wrists.

"Don't," she said. He said nothing, only looked at her. "Please don't? Pretty please?"

"You're not bad at begging."

"How much begging would I have to do to get you naked?"

"Am I naked yet?"

"Not completely."

"Then obviously you need to beg more." Chris took her naked breasts in both of his hands and held them, squeezing them lightly and massaging them. "Don't you?"

She couldn't quite believe it. This was Chris Steffensen? The Chris Steffensen who only worked up the courage to kiss her after they'd gotten into the parental whiskey stash that night? The Chris who'd barely spoken in school except to his closest friends and even then never said more than necessary? He'd walked down the halls, face half-hidden by long blond hair, didn't talk in class, didn't put himself in anyone's way and only really expressed himself with his fists when someone went after Dillon. How had that shy, quiet, intense teenage boy turned into this strong, confident, beautiful man? Ten years had been very kind to Chris. She could get used to being with a man like him.

"Please take your clothes off," she said. "All of them. I want to see your body, because if the rest of it is as good as what I've already seen, I'm going to be the luckiest woman on earth tonight. And I've never been the luckiest woman on earth, and after the past couple of days, I think I've earned it. And even if I haven't, I want it, anyway. Also…your cock is sexy as hell and I want to feel it on me and in me. If I need to earn it some way, just say the word."

"The word."

"You aren't cocky. You're arrogant."

"Why is my cock not in your mouth? I could have sworn it was cocksucking time."

"What time is it?" she asked.

He looked up at the clock on the wall over the wood-stove.

"Ten fourteen."

"It's after cocksucking time," she said. "Allow me to apologize for my tardiness."

"Actions speak louder than words."

Joey didn't say another word. It was the sexiest thing she'd ever seen a man do in her life—pull down his pants to show her his cock after she'd made a "little cocky" remark. Sexy and smug and smoldering. He hadn't said a word. He didn't need to. He was big enough to impress her, and he'd known it. Quiet Chris. Shy Chris. Sweet, sensitive Chris. Had he always had this side to him even in high school? If she'd seen past the chain wallet, the long hair, the brooding silences, the drugs, maybe he would have been her first time instead of just her first kiss.

"You want to lie down?" she asked.

He shook his head no.

"No?"

"Didn't your friend tell you the best way to get over one guy was to get under another?"

"I don't know if she meant it that literally."

"I'm taking it that literally. Stay on your back. I'll come to you."

"And on me?"

"Not yet. But maybe later."

"If I'm good?"

"Now you're learning."

She stretched out on her back again. Chris stood up off the bed but only long enough to finishing undressing. Jeans off. Boxer briefs off. Wearing nothing but the slightest smile, he crawled back over her, took her wrists in his hands and pushed them over her head onto the bed. She lay there, panting, aroused, scared in all the best ways to be scared, the ways people courted danger by skydiving and having sex with near-strangers. But this felt safe, too, safe as a roller coaster. Controlled fear. Chris wasn't a stranger even if he seemed like it when he acted like this. She'd known him since she was twelve and although years had passed since she and he had been friends, it didn't matter. He was one of the good guys. Dillon made it out of high school alive and well thanks to Chris. Now she'd thank him personally.

"You can tell me no to anything," he said as he straddled her chest with his knees. "You shouldn't. But you can."

"I don't want to tell you no. I don't want to tell you anything."

"Why not?"

"I want you to put my mouth to better use."

He laughed a genuine laugh, not sexy, just honest. Just a laugh.

With his hands still on her wrists and holding her lightly down on the bed, he bent down and kissed her on the lips.

Against them, he said, "I used to dream about being your first in high school. I didn't tell Dillon that part of my crush."

"You don't get to be my first time. But maybe you can be the best time?"

"That's a lot of pressure."

"I don't know. So far so good."

"Your ex wasn't that good in bed?"

"He was fantastic in bed."

He got the compliment. She could tell from the way he inhaled, like he felt the words as much as heard them. Chris released her wrist. He cupped the back of her neck to lift her so he could unhook her bra and remove it completely. It ended up with his clothes on the floor. She hoped she wouldn't be seeing it again for many, many hours. Or ever.

Chris unbuttoned the top button of her jeans and he paused for a split second as if waiting for her to object. She had no objections. None. Instead of raising an objection, she raised her hips, allowing him to slide her jeans down her legs and off her. She was glad she'd taken the time to shave her legs in the shower. Once Kira planted that "jump him" seed in her brain, it had taken root. When he started to peel her underwear off, she knew it was going to happen and she was happy about it. She wanted this. No fear, no nervousness, no guilt. Only pleasure. As it should be.

Chris pressed a kiss onto her stomach. She dug her hands in his hair—such soft hair—and sighed as his lips left a burning trail from hip to hip and then down and down a little more.

"I thought it was your turn first," she said as he kissed her upper thighs. He pushed her legs open.

"It's our turn."

"Our turn?"

In one impressively smooth movement, Chris turned around, straddled her shoulders and dropped his head between her legs. She lifted her head and took his cock into her mouth as he ran his tongue lightly up and down the seam of her vulva. Moaning, she opened her legs even wider for him and took more of him into her mouth. She gripped the back of his thighs and found them hard as steel in her hands. And he was hard as steel between her lips. The only thing soft was the kiss he placed on her clitoris. A gentle kiss followed by a lick and another lick. He spread her wider with his fingertips and licked her deeper inside. It felt so good she moaned, and since Chris's cock was deep in her mouth he moaned, too. More of a groan than a moan. Whatever it was, Joey was pretty sure she'd never heard a man make a sound that sexy and sensual.

As she sucked him, she ran her hands up and down the backs of his legs, grabbing his ass a few times to playfully distract him and to drag him down closer to her. He got the hint and started pushing his hips in and out, fucking her mouth. He didn't go too hard or too fast, didn't choke her with his cock, which she appreciated. He was careful even as he went down on her, taking his time, teasing her with kisses and making her work for more by spreading wider for him and pulling her knees up to her chest.

"Beautiful," Chris said as he caressed her wet open body with his fingertips. She could feel it as he massaged her inner labia, opening them up, and circling her vagina over and over again.

"In, please," she said.

"What did you say?"

"You know what I said."

"Say it again."

"I said, 'In, please.' Go inside me. Please."

"Well…since you said please."

He pushed one finger into her and her hips came off the bed in embarrassing eagerness for more. He pushed in a second finger and licked her clitoris again.

"I can't…" she panted.

"What?"

"I can't suck your cock when you're doing that. It feels too good. We can either six or nine but we can't sixty-nine."

"Weak," he said. "Your game is weak."

"I'm sorry!" She dissolved into laughter as Chris climbed off her and stretched out along the side of her body. He fondled her breasts, shaking his head the whole time.

"I'm sorry," she said again. "You made me feel too good, and I couldn't concentrate on what I was doing anymore. And your cock deserves my full concentration."

"That it does."

"Then again, so does my pussy."

"Truer words."

"So what do we do?"

"Flip for it?"

"Flip a coin?" Joey asked.

"I got a quarter."

"Okay, so who's heads and who's tails?"

"Heads I go down on you. Tails you go down on me."

"Or."

"Or what?"

"Or you could fuck me, and we could both enjoy it at the same time?" Seemed like a reasonable suggestion to her.

"Can I tell you a secret?" he asked.

"Tell me anything."

"I only have one condom on me. And I'm in no hurry to get this over with."

"That's not a bad secret."

"You don't have any on you, do you?"

She shook her head. "Sorry. I didn't plan this 'jump on the first guy who offers' thing very well."

"Nothing for it, then. We'll just have to keep foreplaying for at least another hour."

"Oh. Darn."

"Real shame, isn't it?" Chris said.

"A damn shame."

"Keep telling me how much of a shame it is while I eat your pussy."

"What happened to the coin flip?"

"I won it."

"I don't remember—"

Before she could finish telling him she had no memory at all of this supposed coin flip of his, it was too late. He had already slid between her legs again and opened her up for him. Once more he pushed two fingers inside of her, easing them in and out and around the warm, wet interior of her body as he licked her and sucked her and kissed her and finger-fucked her. She was awash in pleasure, in that sort of soft liquid pleasure that suffuses the stomach and back and hips all at once and makes the thighs tense and quiver and fingers clutch at the sheets. That sort of pleasure.

She was going to come and soon and hard and on his mouth. Joey's head fell back and her shoulders came off the bed again. Sweat beaded on her forehead, and she dug her heels into the mattress as Chris brought her to the pinnacle of pleasure and left her there as he slowed down, eased up the pressure to draw it out a little longer…a little longer…

"Please, Chris," she said between labored breaths.

"Not yet."

He stopped licking her and just used his fingers inside her. She'd been close to coming and now the urge faded, but only slightly. He hadn't been kidding about wanting to drag the sex out as long as possible. He brought her almost to coming again and she could have screamed and would have if it didn't feel so good getting there and back again.

"I'm dying," she whispered. Her lips were dry and her lungs burned.

"I'll let you come this time. Maybe."

"Are you trying to kill me?"

"You think I'm in any hurry to be done here? Do you have any idea how good you taste and how sexy you are like this?"

"Like this" was sweaty, flushed, writhing on the bed with her legs open as wide as possible and his head between her thighs and his fingers deep inside her. Maybe he was right. She did feel sexy like this. The only person in the room sexier was Chris, who seemed to have fallen madly in love with her vulva and couldn't seem to stop kissing it. His beard tickled her inner thighs and she wondered if Kira was right about the beard burn. Was that really a thing? Well, she'd probably find out before morning. Even if it was a thing and even if it hurt like hell tomorrow…oh, it was worth it. So worth it.

"Chris," she said.

"Joey."

"Please give me an orgasm. I don't ask for much. But I do ask for that. I beg for it."

"Will you say my name when you come?"

"If that's the price I have to pay."

"It is."

"Then yes. I was planning on doing that, anyway."

"My name. Not your ex's."

"I have an ex? Weird. I can't remember any ex. I thought it was just you and me in the world."

Chris chuckled. "Your game isn't as weak as I thought."

"Chris," she said. "Chris."

"What?"

"Just practicing."

"You're amazing," he said. "And so is your body. And so is your pussy. I'm so glad to finally meet it."

He wrapped his lips around her clitoris and sucked it and licked it as once more he brought her to the edge of climaxing. She lifted her head off the bed and watched him as he kissed her. His eyes were closed and he looked intent on his work and yet…sublime. This was not a man who went down on her begrudgingly or only to get a blow job out of her. This was a man who loved doing what he was doing and it showed.

"You're gorgeous," she said.

He opened his eyes—blue eyes—and raised his chin.

"Lie down and come," he said. "You can tell me how pretty I am later."

She lay down. These were orders she could get used to following.

With both hands, Chris spread her wet folds open and with the flat of his tongue lapped at her clitoris in long slow licks that turned into short fast licks until she was frozen on the bed, paralyzed but with the sharpest, most intense sensation of pleasure she could remember feeling in all her life. And it went on and on, waves of it hitting her like ocean waves. Not gently, but hard, knocking her under, slamming the breath out of her. Her hips bucked and her vagina contracted on Chris's fingers. She didn't scream his name. She didn't have the breath or energy to scream. But she sighed it, moaned it, and when her orgasm subsided and Chris climbed up to lie at her side, she said it again.

"Chris." She met his eyes.

"Joey."

"That felt amazing. My vagina is smiling."

"Seriously?"

He pushed her legs open, looked down at her and back at her face.

"Oh, shit, it is. I've never seen that before."

Joey put her hands on her face and laughed behind them.

"No. No hiding your face. I need that face." Chris took her wrists and removed her hands from her face.

"You need my face?"

"Yes."

"For what?"

"I'm going to fuck it."

"Oh," she said. "Well, in that case, go right ahead."

"Don't mind if I do."

Chris leaned over and with his hand on himself guided his cock back into her mouth. She took it in eagerly, wanting to return even a fraction of the pleasure he'd given her. He needed to come and she wanted him to come. In her mouth, on her breasts, she didn't care. But making him come as hard as he'd made her was Joey's highest priority tonight.

There wasn't much in the world she found sexier than the way a man moved his hips while fucking. It was one reason she liked a light on during sex. Now she had a front row seat to the action. Chris moved with a slow steady rhythm as he fucked her mouth, his stomach taut with tension. He didn't piston his hips, no jackhammering her mouth. Carefully he pushed. Carefully he pulled out. All the while he breathed heavily, half groaning with each thrust in, inhaling sharply each time he withdrew from her mouth. His hands gripped the sheets above her head and Joey ran her hands up his arms. They were tense, so tense. His entire body felt tense against her hands. He was hard everywhere, and she loved his hardness, especially the hardness in her mouth. With her fingernails she dug into the backs of his thighs and scratched downward, not breaking the skin but making sure he felt it, really felt it. The moan he made was obscene. She wished she could have recorded it. It would have been her new ringtone, and maybe then she'd actually like it when someone called her.

Joey would have told him to come but she couldn't talk at the moment. She lifted her head instead and took him even deeper into her mouth. Maybe that would give him the hint she wasn't going to stop until he came. He seemed to get the hint because he started to move a little harder and faster in her mouth. He was still careful not to choke her but she could tell it was getting more difficult for him to go slowly. Good. Let him let go. Let him fuck her hard. She didn't care. She wanted it. It was delicious, decadent, dirty and distracting. And sexy. So damn sexy.

Chris panted hard, loudly. She loved the sound of his pleasure and the taste of his cock and the scent of his arousal. This was exactly what she needed—sex that was nothing but sex. No love, no relationship, no pressure, no pain. All bodies, no hearts. Just pure unadulterated fucking.

With a low grunt, Chris came in her mouth, filling it as she swallowed as best she could. He gave another grunt, and this one sounded almost like pain. He pulled out of her mouth and collapsed next to her on his back.

"Fuck…" He rubbed his face as she wiped her mouth with the back of her hand. "That felt so good it hurt."

"Best kind of pain."

"God, yes." He looked over at her and grinned. "Stay there."

"I'm naked. Where would I go?"

He didn't answer as he walked from the room, still naked himself. Chris should do that more often—walk out of rooms naked. The view was spectacular. Better than the view of the mountain from her window. She should charge money for a view like that.

Chris returned quickly with a glass of water and a glass of wine.

"Pick one," he said.

"I get to pick?"

"You're the one with the mouth full of my come."

"I swallowed it. Most of it."

"Take the water," he said. "We'll share the wine."

She took the water from him and drank it down gratefully.

Meanwhile Chris sipped at the red wine, a pinot noir she'd found in the fridge. Pinot was her favorite. No way Chris could have known that. She didn't drink wine in high school. Dillon must have put it there.

"I feel kind of weird fucking in this house," she said. "It was my parents' house. They fucked in this house. Not us."

"Dillon fucked in this house."

"What?"

She sat up and looked down at him.

"If you're gay and in high school and scared about being outed, wouldn't you go as far away as you could for your dates?"

"Well…yeah. But I didn't know he brought guys out here."

"Just the one guy. Trevor? I think that was his name."

"Trevor? I don't remember a Trevor."

"He didn't go to our school. They met at the Ski Bowl."

"How do you know all this and I don't?"

"He might be gay but he's still a dude. A guy doesn't want to tell his baby sister about his sex life."

"But he wanted to tell you?"

"I covered for him. When he and Trevor were out here, he was supposedly crashing at my house."

"I'm stunned. I'm just stunned. And jealous. Why did he get to fuck out here and I didn't?"

"I would have fucked you out here. But you weren't into me."

"My mistake," she said, rolling onto her side to face him. "I kind of regret that now."

He laid a hand on her naked hip and caressed it.

"I wish… I wish I hadn't been such a coward. I could have told you."

"I wish I hadn't been such a snob. I don't know if you telling me would have made a difference. You were my brother's stoner friend. And I liked you. I did. I liked that you were so protective of Dillon. I liked hanging out with you. I didn't *like you* like you. Except for the night you kissed me. Then I liked you."

"We were drunk. Doesn't count."

"No, I guess not. But I'm very sober tonight. And tonight counts."

"You don't like me. I'm just the rebound guy."

"I like you. You're very sexy when you're not stoned."

"I haven't gotten stoned since my freshman year in college."

"You said you went to a trade school."

"Because I flunked out of college."

"Because of the pot?"

"Because of the pot and the drinking and the not giving enough of a shit to go to class. When I flunked out,

Dad kicked me out. Mom un-kicked me out. Sort of. She said I could stay in the storage room over the garage for six months but after that it was either go back to school or move out for real."

"So you got a job?"

"I had to clean up the room in the garage first. Dad kept all his tools out there." He stopped and smiled. "This will sound dumb."

"Sound dumb. I want to hear you sound dumb."

"I found a knife, a really pretty one, and Dad had some birch wood he'd never gotten around to using for something. And I was bored. I started whittling it. It made me feel better, better than I'd felt in a long time. Clear up here." He tapped his forehead. "I did that for a couple weeks. Played with Dad's tools, whittled, carved a little. In shop class in high school, I'd made a chair. I taught myself how to make one again, a rocking chair this time, and gave it to Mom as a thank-you for un-kicking me out. She thought it was so pretty she cried. Dad had been promising her a porch rocker for years like the one her grandmother had. Right after that, Dad had a heart attack and had to cut way back on work. I stepped up because I knew I could do it then. Making one stupid chair changed me. Yeah, that did sound dumb."

"No, it sounds kind of…spiritual, maybe?" She hoped that didn't sound as cheesy to him as it sounded to her.

"It's wild, you know. Trees are alive and they die when you cut them down, but if you treat the wood the right way, carve it, stain it, polish it, make something beautiful out of it, or something useful—"

"Like a rocking chair for your mom?"

"Right. If you make something out of that wood, if you use it well, it'll last for centuries. It'll last longer than the tree might have lived. How's that for an afterlife?"

"Sounds like a good afterlife to me. So making a chair changed you. I like that."

"You make your mother cry by giving her something you made with your own hands and it gets to you, you know? That's when I decided to get my act together. I quit drugs, all of them. I'm clean now. Have been for years."

Joey felt an unexpected knot in her throat. She hadn't meant to see Chris's heart like that. She hadn't meant to go digging. She certainly hadn't expected to hit gold like she had.

"Anybody ever tell you that you clean up really nice?"

"Dillon did. But he doesn't count."

"Why not?"

"Because right now, only you count."

He kissed her again, gently, but she didn't want that. No gentle kisses for her. She needed rough and hard. She needed bruising kisses that would remind her tomorrow that she was single and could do stuff like have wild meaningless one-night stands with old high school friends. Of course, if Chris kept making her feel this good, this sexy, she might accidentally find a little meaning in it and that would be terrible, wouldn't it? She didn't want to have to get over two guys in one month. That was a lot of rebounding.

Joey touched his face tenderly. He pulled back and looked her in the eyes.

"What is it?" he asked, his voice soft and low. His eyelashes were long and they made him look younger in the low lamplight. They made him look almost innocent.

She didn't want to hurt him.

Wait. Where had that thought come from? That she didn't want to hurt him? He was half a foot taller than her, fifty pounds heavier, stronger, a man who rebuilt houses for his work. How could she hurt him? And yet the thought persisted.

"Nothing. I just like the beard."

"I want to be inside you now."

"You can be inside me now."

Chris cupped her between her legs and pushed two and then three fingers inside her. Joey gripped his shoulder as he moved his hand with a deep spiraling motion in and out of her, opening her back up for him. She wanted to be open for him. She spread her legs wider.

"You feel so good inside," he said. "You're so wet."

"You made me this wet. We haven't even fucked yet and there's a wet spot underneath me."

"You're so sexy when you come. Your whole body was into it. I've never seen a girl move like that. I'm hard again just thinking about it. I want you to move like that on my cock."

"Then put your cock in me and I will."

"Stay here. I need to get the condom."

"Where'd you leave your wallet?"

"It's not in my wallet." He kissed the tip of her nose.

"Where is it, then?" she asked, narrowing her eyes in suspicion.

"In my toolbox."

A man who stored his condoms in his toolbox. That

was cute. Very cute. She could get used to being with a guy like this.

Except she couldn't get used to it.

Because she was leaving right after the wedding.

Because she was on the rebound, and if she got used to this, she'd just get hurt again.

This time when he walked naked from the room, she didn't let herself enjoy the view.

5

HOLY.

Fucking.

Shit.

What the hell was he doing?

This was not the plan. Why wasn't it the plan? This was a much better plan than the original plan.

Chris leaned back against the door in the master bedroom—the only part of the room without fresh paint on it—and closed his eyes. He breathed, breathed again.

The plan was to be here when Joey arrived so he could talk to Joey.

He wasn't talking to Joey. He was having sex with Joey.

Joey.

Joey Silvia. Joey Silvia, who he'd been in love with in high school and pined for even after he graduated, even after he'd heard she'd gone to the University of Hawaii instead of somewhere he could actually hope to see her every now and then like the University of Oregon. She could have been a Duck. And there was always OSU.

Why hadn't she gone to Oregon State? She could have been a Beaver. What girl didn't want to be a Beaver?

He peeled his body off the door and rummaged through his toolbox for the condom he kept in a box in the bottom. Shortly after opening his own contracting business, he'd discovered that lots of his clients were women—single and divorced—who'd never been taught anything about home repair. More than once he'd been propositioned by a beautiful newly divorced lady on the rebound. More than once he'd succumbed to the temptation. Three times precisely, with three different divorced women who were setting up their new homes and needed a handyman to be, well, handy. And he'd been handy. Very, very handy.

But being with Joey felt nothing like that.

Those few late-afternoon assignations had been nothing but sex. Good sex, more or less. But still just sex. Only his body had been there, not him. Not the real him that you only showed to someone after a few weeks together, a few months. With Joey, he'd shown up right then and there, right out of the gate. He'd ordered her around, talked dirty, "made her" lie on her back and suck him off. Usually he never did that sort of thing until he was in a relationship with someone and felt comfortable enough to talk about that side of him. Never had he been this himself with a girl the first time. Never had he felt that safe, that comfortable, to do it when he was with a stranger. Because Joey wasn't a stranger. Because he'd known her for years, since he and Dillon were freshman in high school together and sixth-grader Joey tagged along when they'd gone to movies or the skate park. He didn't care. She was less annoying than Dillon, anyway. Then by the time she started high school, it was a whole different game. On the first day of school she showed up in Dillon's car. She wore tight jeans, a low-cut shirt, a scarf draped around her neck, and instead of her usual ponytail, she wore her long straight dark hair down and over her shoulder. And she smelled like vanilla, like cookies out of the oven, and he wanted to devour her, which—as a teenage boy—just meant making out with her for a few years until she warmed up to the idea of sex and then having sex for a few more years until his cock broke off from all the sex they'd had and they were forced to be just friends. Friends who made out. It sounded like a good plan to him. He even told it to Dillon while they were getting high in the garage one night their senior year.

It was a pipe dream. Literally. He could only talk about how crazy he was about Joey when he was smoking weed. But he didn't have any drugs to blame or thank for this trip. It was real. He had Joey in the bedroom waiting for him to fuck her. What was he waiting for?

"Dillon is going to kill me." He sighed to himself as he opened the bedroom door, the condom in his hand. He stood in the doorway to the second bedroom. Joey lay on her stomach, her feet in the air, her head on a pillow. She stared out the window into the deep wet green forest outside the house.

"Isn't it beautiful here?" she asked. "I'd almost forgotten how beautiful it is out here. Like Narnia. I love the moss. That's my favorite part. Did you ever notice how the tree branches look like giant green tarantulas when they're all bunched together and covered in moss?"

Chris couldn't speak at first. She looked so comfortable on the bed he'd made, so lovely with her black hair lying over her soft brown skin, the lamplight turning it golden.

Yeah, okay, so Dillon might kill him for having a one-night stand with his sister. So what? That woman on that bed was worth dying for. His cock told him so.

"I hadn't noticed that," he said as he slid onto the bed next to her and threw his leg over her lower back. "But now that you mention it…"

The moss-covered trees outside the window did look a little like furry spider legs.

"You have beautiful eyes," he said, rubbing her shoulders.

"They're just brown."

"No, I mean, the way you see things."

She rolled over onto her back. "I see you."

"What do you see?"

"Someone with a lot going on in here…" She tapped his forehead. "Even when there's not much coming out of here." She caressed his lips.

"Are you accusing me of being a thinker? That's a new one."

"I'm accusing you of having more to you than meets the eye. You say I have good eyes. How did I not see you had this person inside you?"

"We were in high school. What did we know?"

"You liked me. I should have liked you."

"I didn't give you a lot to like. And I would have been an idiot to not want you. And I might have been a stoner and a slacker—to quote Dad—but I wasn't an idiot."

"No, definitely not that. Not then, not now."

"I'm in bed with you. I'm definitely the smartest man alive."

"I am also clearly a genius." She leaned into him, wrapped her arms around his shoulders. Her skin was so soft and smooth and warm to the touch. He could stay in this bed forever as long as she stayed with him.

He kissed her because he had to, because he wanted to so much that if he didn't he'd never forgive himself. He had enough on his conscience. He didn't need more.

Chris pushed her onto her back and kissed her neck, her chest... Joey arched her back and he knew she wanted her nipples sucked again and he was more than happy to do it. Ecstatic even. Really, she was the one doing him the favor here. But first...he had to tease. It was his favorite thing to do in bed—taunt, tease, torment, even torture a little tiny bit. He knelt over her on his hands and knees and kissed her right breast under her nipple. Just under it. As lightly as he could he kissed that soft, soft patch of skin, licked it. Then he kissed and licked around her nipple carefully, tenderly, lightly.

"You're driving me crazy," she said.

"I know."

"I know you know. I just wanted you to know I know you know."

"Tell me what you want."

"I have to say it?"

"Yes..." He breathed the word onto her breast and her nipple hardened.

"I want you to suck my nipples."

"Is that so?"

"It is so and you said—"

He covered her nipple with his mouth and licked it. Abruptly Joey went silent. He massaged her breast with his open mouth for a few delicious moments before latching on to her nipple and sucking. She moaned as he swirled his tongue around the tip and took it into his mouth gently but deeply. Not to be outdone in the torture department, Joey reached between his legs and stroked his erection with her soft little hands. He could tell she was using just her fingertips, barely touching him, almost tickling. It drove him wild. He was hard already but getting harder with every passing second. He caught her wrists and pushed them over her head again, pinning her to the bed.

"Not fair," she pouted. God, he loved it when women pouted like that—*Yes, please, act like I'm the meanest man in the world for not letting you stroke me off. I will reward that pout in ways you can't even imagine...*

"Life isn't fair, little girl. You lie there under me and behave yourself like I told you to and when you're allowed to rub my cock I'll tell you."

"Am I allowed to rub your cock right now?"

"No. You're allowed to lie there while I fuck you. I'm going to fuck you right now. Unless you want to pout some more."

"Nope. I'm good. I'm all done pouting."

Jesus, did he just call her "little girl"? He did have it bad for her already. Already or still or something like that. Didn't matter. He wasn't going to think about how much he'd kick himself for doing this tomorrow when he realized he'd had the sexiest sex of his life with a woman he wouldn't see again for years. If ever.

He sat up and rolled on the condom. Joey watched. Did she know how hot that was? Being watched while he touched himself?

"I wanted to be an astronaut when I was a kid," he said.

"That was out of left field. Like way left field." Joey smiled, which was a good reaction to his non sequitur.

"There's a point to that comment."

"I can't wait to hear it."

Chris kneed her thighs apart and lowered himself onto her. With one hand he braced himself over her. With the other he guided his cock to the entrance of her vagina.

"Every kid wants to be an astronaut," he said, talking to keep himself from coming immediately. Fuck, he was doing it. Joey. Inside Joey. "But kids don't get to be astronauts and they grow up and they're doctors or lawyers or plumbers or nannies or whatever. I dreamed of being with you when I was a kid. And it's like…"

"Like what?" Joey dug her heels into the bed and lifted her hips to take him inside her. He let her, didn't try to stop her, let her work her pelvis so she was bringing herself around him instead of him thrusting into her. That would come later.

"Like I dreamed of being an astronaut as a kid and then I grew up and didn't give that dream a second thought because what grown man with his own business still goes around dreaming of being an astronaut? And then one random day, years after you give up on that dream, NASA shows up and says, 'Hey, congrats, you get to be an astronaut now. Let's go.' I'd forgotten I had that dream, but you better believe I'd be on the next rocket to space."

Joey lifted her arms, wrapped them around his neck and brought him down onto her body.

"That's the sweetest, weirdest compliment a man has ever given me." She kissed his mouth and he had to make himself stop smiling to kiss her back.

"Yeah, well…all the blood is in my cock right now. I blame the weird on that."

"What do you blame the sweet on?"

"On you, Joey."

He thrust into her then, a smooth hard stroke that went deep. Joey sighed with unmistakable pleasure. Of all the sounds that a woman made during sex, his favorite was the sound of relief when he finally penetrated her. Like she'd been waiting for this moment, and *finally...thank God*, he was inside her. He knew how she felt. He pulled out an inch or two and pushed back in, finding his groove, his best angle to move in her. Even with the condom on he could feel her wetness surrounding him and her heat, her incredible heat. Beneath him she moved in slow undulations, lifting and circling her hips, circling and spiraling, spiraling and pushing. Chris listened to her breaths—ragged and shallow. She licked her lips and her head fell back when he pushed in deeper.

"Open wider for me, babe," he said into her ear.

Joey lifted her knees and splayed them open.

"I like that," she said.

"Good angle?" He pushed in again, pulled out, pushed in and in...

"I like that you called me babe."

"I liked that you liked it."

"We're a good team."

"Yes, yes, we are."

Chris shifted so that he was on his knees and hands and could move his hips more freely. He rolled his pelvis against hers, not pulling out but staying inside her as he moved. Her clitoris needed as much attention as her vagina and at this angle he could graze that sensitive skin with every thrust. Joey gasped as he hit in just the right spot.

"You liked that."

"I did…" she breathed. "Do it again…"

"Say the magic word."

"Please?"

"That's the magic word."

He shifted again and thrust. Once more she gasped, twitched, shuddered and moaned. In high school she seemed so untouchable, so young and innocent. Didn't stop him from having obscene sexual fantasies about her, but even back then he hadn't believed they'd ever come true. But this woman was made of passion. This was a woman who adored sex. There was no faking pleasure like this. He could see it in her eyes, in the way she looked up at him under the veil of her eyelashes. And her wetness was incredible. Her inner muscles clenched around him with each thrust. She was enjoying this. Maybe as much as he was—but he wouldn't bet money on it.

Chris bent his head to suck her nipples again. They felt perfect in his mouth. Her breasts were his ideal—not too big, not too small, a perfect handful with reddish-brown nipples he couldn't get enough of.

"You're a breast man, aren't you?" she asked, her voice hardly a whisper.

"I am," he readily confessed. "Ass is nice, but tits are the tits."

"Don't make me laugh while you're fucking me. I once laughed a guy right out of my vagina."

"I dare you to try. I'm not going anywhere. I'm in and I plan on staying…" He thrust in deep. "Right." He thrust in deeper. "Here." He thrust in as deep as he could go before pulling out again to the tip.

"So good." Joey wrapped her legs around him, tucking them against his sides and resting her heels on his back. "Kira says it takes six months at least to rebound from a bad breakup."

"You want me to fuck you for the next six months?"

"Solid," she said. "Non stop."

"I don't know if one condom's going to last six straight months. Better go to Costco."

"That's what oral is for."

"If you think I wouldn't spend half a year eating you out, you don't know me."

"I don't know you. Not anymore. But I'm enjoying getting to know you."

"A pleasure to make your reacquaintance, Joey Silvia."

"The pleasure is all mine…"

Joey raised her head and kissed his naked shoulder. It was a small thing but felt so good he swore an electric current passed from her lips to his shoulder all the way down to his toes and back up to his cock. She kissed his shoulder again, licked and bit it. She liked his shoulders. She liked his body. He could tell because she couldn't seem to stop touching him. Her hands wandered down his arms, down his back, up his sides and his neck and over his chest. She kissed him everywhere she could reach. He had to block out the pleasure of her touches and kisses as he fucked her or he would come in the next fifteen seconds when he wanted to last another fifteen minutes at least. Or another fifteen hours. Fuck it, he'd stay in her the next fifteen weeks. Who needed to work when he had a girl like this willing to spread for him?

One time isn't going to be enough.

He didn't say that out loud, did he?

Chris looked down at Joey's face. Her eyes were

closed. She looked utterly lost in the moment. Good. He hadn't said it out loud. But it was true. One time fucking this woman was a few thousand times too few.

"How you doing?" He whispered the question into her ear between kisses on her neck.

"I need to come," she said.

"Tell me what I can do to make that happen."

"Can you use your fingers on my clit? Please?"

He spread his knees and dragged her down the bed closer to him. He licked his fingertips and pushed them against her swollen clitoris.

"God…"

"Good things happen when you use the magic word."

Now he barely moved in her, just shallow thrusts moving only a couple inches in and out while he massaged her with her fingers. Joey reached up and grasped his shoulders, squeezing them as she neared climax. Her hips bounced on the bed as she coaxed herself toward her orgasm, and he did everything he could to get her there. He rubbed and stroked and worked his cock in her. Her fingers dug so hard into his arms that she nearly broke the skin. Fine. Good. Let her do it. He loved making her feel this good. If he had to bleed a little for it, all the better. He'd have souvenirs to look at in the mirror tomorrow as he remembered every single thing they did to each other this night.

"Come for me, Joey. I want to watch you come. I want to feel it on my cock. I want to feel your pussy squeeze me out. It won't work, but I want to feel it try."

He thrust faster and rubbed harder. She was so wet now he could feel it on his upper thighs, feel it on the bed under them, dripping where they joined. God, it was dirty and beautiful and sexy as hell. This woman—

he could fuck her till he died, which might not be long from now because if she didn't come soon, it would kill him. The need to ride her and slam into her nearly over-whelmed him. Just the thought of it made him thrust a little harder.

"Yes," Joey gasped. "Again."

He thrust in harder. Harder.

"Don't stop."

He grabbed her by the waist and gave it to her, gave her all he had. He pounded into her, cock ramming deep and rough, and she loved it, she fucking loved it. He didn't need her words to tell him, although they did. She said his name, over and over again, called out for more, for it harder, for it faster, and he did it all not be-cause she told him to, but because he needed it as badly as she did. Joey went silent, completely silent, and her back arched so hard her shoulders came completely off the bed. She was coming. He could feel her pussy clenching wildly around him. He rammed her again, slamming into her, holding on to her breasts with both of his hands, squeezing them as he fucked her. And then he came, too, came hard, came harder than he remembered coming in years. Chris felt it behind his eyes, a white light that obliterated the world except for his body, Joey's body and semen that shot out of him in waves of pure sensation.

Slowly he came back to awareness. Wincing, he gen-tly pulled out of Joey, hoping not to lose the condom in the withdrawal. He'd fucked her so hard he had a quick moment of panic that he might have broken it. He couldn't feel it. Then again, he couldn't feel his feet, either, and they were still there. He hoped.

The condom was still there, too, thank fuck. He dropped a kiss on the center of Joey's panting chest.

"I'll be right back," he promised. He left her on the bed and walked into the bathroom. He disposed of the condom, splashed water on his face, peed like usual. Nice that the plumbing still worked after all the rough treatment he'd just put it through.

"Good job," he said to his cock. They were a good team, too.

Chris knew he should probably head out, leave Joey to get comfortable in her new temporary home, but he couldn't help but hope she'd want him to stay the night. Maybe he could tempt her with the promise of breakfast at the Lost Lake Café tomorrow morning. Maybe he could tempt her with the promise of more sex before breakfast. Or after. But preferably before. They didn't have any other condoms but who needed them when they had fingers and tongues and lips?

But first he had to tell her about Lost Lake Village Rentals, which was the one thing he was *supposed* to do with Joey tonight. Dillon had said Joey would be more open to the idea if it came from Chris instead of her own brother. Maybe if Chris could talk Joey into giving their idea a try, Dillon wouldn't kill him for sleeping with her before anything was decided.

And if Joey said yes…that would mean she'd be around here, living here, in Lost Lake or at least near Lost Lake. Chris could see her all the time. It wouldn't mean years until their paths crossed again. He fully intended for their paths to cross again and hard. Joey had such beautiful paths…

He slipped back into the bedroom.

"Hey, Jo. I meant to tell you—"

Chris stopped speaking when he noticed Joey was no longer in the bedroom. She must have gone downstairs while he'd been in the bathroom. Should he wait? Had she run down to use the half bath off the kitchen? Or was she hungry and digging for food, which meant he should definitely join her?

Although they'd just spent the last hour naked together, Chris didn't feel comfortable yet walking around the house without any clothes on. And it looked like she'd dressed, too. Her clothes weren't on the floor anymore where he remembered tossing them. He grabbed his jeans and pulled them on, found his flannel and buttoned it up.

"Jo?" He headed down the steps in bare feet. "Where'd you go?"

"Just down on the couch," she said. Her voice sounded light, but tense, like she was trying to sound happy.

"You okay?"

"Fine. Just tired. Lots of traveling. Jet lag and all that."

Chris walked to the couch and found her wrapped up in a wool blanket, her knees pulled to her chest, a cup of tea clutched tight in her hands.

"Want me to light the fire for you?"

"No, it's okay. I'll go to bed soon."

Chris didn't know what to do, what to say. He sat on the end of the couch, not too far but not too close.

"Do you…feel weird about—?" It was as far as Chris made it in his question before Joey's head dropped to her knees and he heard the unmistakable sound of tears.

"Fuck, Joey, what's wrong?" He moved in closer, terrified to touch her when she was so clearly upset and yet desperate to be near her.

"I'm sorry." She choked out the words between soft sobbing breaths. "It's not you, I swear."

"What is it?"

She raised her head and rubbed tears off her cheeks on the corner of the blanket.

"It's really over."

"What is?"

"Me and Ben."

"Yeah, I assumed it was."

"No, you don't get it. I've never cheated on any guy in my life. I wouldn't. And you and I had sex. And since we did, that means I know it's over, because I wouldn't have sex with someone else if it wasn't. I guess... I guess it just hit me that it's *over* over."

"You want it to be over, right? I mean, he's married."

"Yes, I definitely don't want to date a married man. I don't. But for two years I didn't know he was married. For two years he was just my boyfriend. Mine. All mine. I thought."

"You lost a lot here. You lost your boyfriend and you lost your whole vision of who you thought he was."

"I'm just so stupid. How could I not know? Of course he was married. He never wanted me to come to LA? Never? Not once? Like what did I think that was about? He thought I'd break up with him because the traffic's so bad? Seriously—what was I thinking?"

"I dated a girl for two years without meeting her parents. It just never worked out time-wise with our schedules. It wasn't like she secretly kept her parents chained up in the basement. You just took him at his word. You wanted to believe you were dating an honest man. You wanted to believe the best in someone. That's not stupid."

"It feels stupid. It feels like I'm stupid."

"You aren't. You're a good person who got lied to. We all get lied to. My ex cheated on me two months with her new boyfriend before I figured it out."

"Two months is not two years."

"But she lied to me, and I believed it. You just dated a really good liar."

"His poor wife—she must hate me."

"If she's a good person, she hates him, not you."

"Unless he lied to her."

"That's not your problem. Their marriage is not your problem."

"No," she said softly. "I've got my own problems."

"Work?"

She nodded.

"He's the VP of Operations at the airline. He's not my boss but he is a boss. I can't…but I have to go back. I can't let him win. He should quit, not me. I shouldn't be the one who has to give up her job because he lied."

"Yeah, he should quit. It would be the only honorable thing he could do." Not for one second did Chris think this asshole Ben would quit his job just so Joey could keep working there with some comfort and dignity. A man like that didn't know the meaning of the word *honor*.

"I'm so tempted to call HR on him. You know there's a rule against bosses dating underlings. We ignored it because he wasn't my boss, but if I told them, it would get him fired."

"Do that. Definitely."

"It would probably also get me fired."

"Okay, maybe don't do that. But you should think about, I don't know…"

"What?"

She looked at him with hope in her eyes. Hope and sorrow and enough of both to break his heart and shut him up. Now was not the time to offer her a new job. Now might be the worst time in the history of all time to offer her a new job.

"You should think about yourself," he said. "Just take care of yourself while you're home."

"I will. Thanks, Chris. You're the best."

"Thank you. I know."

That got a little smile out of her.

"I'm going to go to bed," she said, sipping her tea before setting the half-drunk mug down on the coffee table.

"Good idea. I'll just, um, get my boots. Left them upstairs."

He stood up and she smiled at him. He wanted to touch her, caress her face, her hair, something. But she seemed so distant there on the couch wrapped up in her blanket, her body hidden from him, her face wet with tears.

In the bedroom he pulled on his socks and work boots, found his white T-shirt and underwear. He tossed the condom wrapper and straightened the sheets a little so Joey wouldn't have to when she came up to bed. With a pang of regret he looked at the bed where not twenty minutes ago he was buried deep inside Joey and they were having the best sex of their lives. At least, it was some of the best sex of his. What he wouldn't give for a time machine. He'd go back twenty minutes—no, two years—and somehow stop Joey from dating this asshole who'd broken her heart so badly. But that was a childish dream for a grown man. Then again, one dream of his youth had come true tonight. No one could fault him for hoping for another dream come true.

He went back downstairs and Joey was still on the couch. Waiting for him to leave? Probably.

"Hey, I left my number on the nightstand," he said. "Call me or text me or something. I won't take it personally if this was, like, just a one-night thing. But I do want to hear from you. Tell me you're okay or something. Okay?"

"Okay. Thank you."

Thank you? That's what he got after such a sexy, beautiful night? Thank you?

"You can tell your friend now that you did what she suggested. Then maybe she'll get off your back."

"She will. I'll tell her I did exactly what she told me to. Too bad it didn't work."

"Yeah," Chris said, forcing himself to smile. "Too bad."

6

"'Too bad it didn't work'? That's what you said to him?" Kira half screamed the words into the phone. Joey had to hold it out away from her ear to preserve her right ear's hearing.

"Well…yeah."

Joey winced. She hadn't even gotten out of bed before her phone started ringing. Kira, of course, wanted all the details on her night with Chris. At first Kira had been thrilled. Joey had done something naughty for once in her life. She'd slept with a supersexy guy right after meeting—well, re-meeting him—and it had been all that any woman could ever want sex to be. Exciting, sensual, erotic, safe, orgasmic and just good old-fashioned dirty. She should have stopped her story before the end, before she said something incredibly stupid and Chris had left her alone in the cabin, which was actually the last thing she'd wanted.

"You had mind-blowing sex with a hot handyman with a beard and you said, 'Too bad it didn't work' after? Do you know there are over one million words in the English language? There are more words in English than there are in French and German combined. And any of those one million words would have been better than those words. You could have said, 'I like bacon-powered ghost boat parades,' and it would have been a better sentence than that sentence you laid at the feet of that beautiful man and his majestic cock."

"I didn't say it was majestic. It's a dick, not a bald eagle in flight. What I said was that his cock is 'magnificent.' And…can I ask something? Did 'bacon-powered ghost boat parades' really come off the top of your head? Or are you on some sort of drug I need to know about?"

"Joey. This isn't about the ghost boat parades. This is about you and Chris and his magical cock."

"Magnificent. Not magical. It didn't do any tricks. He didn't pull a rabbit out of it."

"He gave you not one but two screaming orgasms in the span of one hour. Sounds like magic to me."

"I'm really not a screamer. It was more like two 'incredibly loud moaning orgasms.' And it was closer to forty-five minutes."

"Can I have him if you don't want him? I'll take a pretty Portland boy with a beard."

"No, you can't have him. He's in Oregon. You are not."

"Fuck LA for a man who said he'd eat your pussy for the next six months. I'll move to Oregon for that. I'm packing my bags right now."

"No, you aren't."

"What if I was?" Kira asked, her voice finally calm again. "What if I did come to Oregon to hang out with you until the wedding? Hmm? What if I did meet this Chris Handyman of yours and he and I hit it off? Would you mind that? Would you mind if he and I got in his big diesel pickup truck and drove off into the sunset?"

"It's Oregon in October. You won't see the sunset. You'll see the fog set. Although that is really pretty."

"You're not answering my question. Would you mind if I came to Lost Lake and went out on a nice dinner date with your handyman and took him back to my cabin and found out just how handy he is? Answer me."

Joey didn't want to answer that question. She didn't want to talk about Chris anymore. Not when she lay in the bed they'd had sex in, on the sheets that still bore the slight warm and spicy scent of his skin, with the wineglass they'd shared still sitting on the nightstand.

"No. I would not like that. But I also wouldn't stop you. He's single. You're single."

"He shouldn't be single, not if he's that good in bed."

"He's that good in bed. And it didn't work. As soon as he left to go to the bathroom after… I just couldn't keep it together. All I could think about was how two years of my life were officially over. I didn't get dumped because he found someone better or because he got a job somewhere else or something. The last two years of my life have been a lie. It might as well have not even happened. It's all a waste. Two years, down the toilet."

"Look, I know breakups are hard. And they're ten times harder when somebody lies or cheats. I know. I've been there. But Ben was not your whole life. You have a job you love that you kick ass at. I was there before you were. I know how much we were making. And I know how much more we made after a year with you in charge of marketing. You're a marketing genius and we all know it. Whether you stay or not, you have two years of work experience, two years of contacts, two years of successes, to put on your résumé. You have friends—me, for example—and what more do you need than me? And you live in fucking Honolulu, Hawaii, so close to the beach you can see actual whales from your apartment window. Can you really tell me that's all down the toilet? Really? Go look. Go look in the toilet and tell me if you see any whales in it."

"Kira…"

"Go. Look. For. Whales. In. Your. Toilet. Right. Now."

Joey laughed. It was the first big good laugh she'd had all day. She needed that.

"I don't have to look. I can tell you there are no whales in my toilet."

"See? It wasn't all a waste, then. And you can stop feeling sorry for yourself any minute now. Ben lied to you. He cheated. That makes him a cheating liar and cheating liars are not worth all the power you're giving him. He doesn't deserve the right to taint the past two years of your life when you and I both know that you had a pretty damn good two years."

"I did. Yes. I absolutely had a good two years."

"Good. Thank you. I needed to hear that. If you flush the past two years down the toilet, you flush me, too. And I don't want to be flushed."

"I won't flush you."

"I can't tell you how relieved I am to hear that. Now, we need to figure out what to do about your handyman."

"He's not my handyman. He's my brother's handyman. And he's probably not Dillon's handyman anymore because everything on the cabin is done. He's doing other jobs this week."

"Anywhere close by?"

"Timber Ridge, I think he said."

"What's that?"

"A hotel-lodge-type place near the top of the mountain, really pretty inside. And it's right at the top of the mountain. Great view. Great skiing. Nice place."

"Maybe you should go skiing. Maybe bump into Chris."

"I doubt I'll find him on the ski slopes."

"You'll find him somewhere up there, right? He left his number?"

"He left his number."

"You could use that number to meet up with him."

"And do what? I tried what you said. Get over one guy by getting under another. I did that. I did it hard. It was awesome. And…it didn't work."

"Try again."

"Kira."

"I'm serious. You know the old saying—if at first you don't succeed, fuck that guy again."

"I don't remember that old saying."

"It's before your time," Kira said.

"Kira, I love you. I do. But I don't think playing around with Chris's feelings is a good way to help me take care of mine. It's not really fair to him."

"Did you ask him?"

"What?"

"Did you ask him his opinion on this? Isn't he older than you?"

"Yeah, he's twenty-eight."

"So he's an adult."

"Right."

"Okay. Then text him. Ask if you can have lunch or dinner with him. Have lunch or dinner with him. Ask him if he'd mind being your bed buddy until you come back to work after the wedding. He might say yes. He might say no. But that's his call, not yours."

"You really—"

"Do you like him?" Kira asked, and for the first time in their entire conversation she sounded one hundred percent sincere. "Chris, that is. Do you like him?"

"I've always liked him. He used to protect Dillon. They were best friends in high school. Dillon got outed and Chris broke at least one nose trying to keep Dillon from getting jumped in the parking lot. Chris was a tough twerp back then. I was always scared he'd get hurt trying to keep Dillon from getting hurt. That's a real friend who will break a nose for you."

"I'd break a nose for you, JoJo."

"I'd break a nose for you, too, KiKi."

"Don't call me that."

"You called me JoJo."

"Are you going to text Chris and at least talk to him about last night?"

"Yes, I'm going to text Chris. I don't want him thinking for one second I regret what happened."

"Then you can call me anything you want."

"I'll call you tonight after I talk to him. How's that?"

"That's perfect. Now go jump that pretty bearded handy boy before I do."

"I'm hanging up now." And Joey did.

For a few more minutes, Joey lay in the bed, the bed Chris made with his own hands. She couldn't deny it was kind of sexy, that he could literally make a bed. And it was such a beautiful bed, beautifully crafted, beautifully situated in a room beautiful enough to deserve such a bed. Hard to believe this cabin was the very same dump her family had lived in during all her summers from age eight to eighteen. Chris really could work magic. For a couple hours last night he'd made her sadness magically go away. It came back but for a while it was gone, and that was quite a trick. And it was almost Halloween, a season for tricks and treats and a little dark magic. Maybe Kira was right. Maybe she should give it another shot with Chris. Even if they didn't have sex again—although they probably would if last night were any indicator—she did like hanging out with him. She felt like a kid again with him. Like as long as Chris were around, she'd be okay. And being okay after a bad breakup was the only kind of Halloween treat she wanted right now.

Joey picked up her phone and wrote a message to Chris. Hey, it's Joey. Thanks for last night. It was pretty amazing until I fucked it up. Will you let me buy you lunch to make it up to you? I'd love to see Timber Ridge, anyway. If not, I understand. I might not want to see me, either.

Without sending the message, she put her phone back on the nightstand next to the wineglass they'd both drunk out of. She looked at it and smiled. Last night had been pretty spectacular. She couldn't believe Chris had that side to him—that commanding, dirty-talking, wicked side. Still waters run deep, right? That's what that saying said? Turns out still waters run deep *and* dirty sometimes. And now that she'd finally seen that deep and dirty side of Chris, she really wanted to see it again. If he didn't mind. If he wasn't pissed at her for her little breakdown she had postsex. Only one way to find out. She hit Send on the message. While she waited for a reply, Joey climbed out of bed, took a quick shower and threw on her clothes.

When she returned to the bedroom, she had two messages—one from Chris and one from Kira.

The one from Chris read, I remember two people fucking last night. I don't remember anybody fucking up. Lunch sounds great. The Green Owl at two?

Joey replied with an immediate, See you there.

Kira's text simply read, Just how magnificent a cock are we talking here?

To which Joey replied, It's a lot like Mount Hood. Big, lovely and you want to spend a long time on it. Except you don't want Mount Hood blowing its load and you do want Chris... This metaphor broke down really quickly.

Then Kira wrote back, I think this Chris guy fucked your brains out.

To which Joey replied, If my brains didn't alert me that I was dating a married man, I'm better off without them.

"I'm GOING TO have to kill you, you know that, right?"

Chris stood up straight and clasped his hands behind his back. He'd seen this coming.

"I understand. I don't make a habit of telling anybody what I do in my private life, but considering, you know—"

"That it was my bedroom? In my bed? And my sister?"

Chris would have preferred to have had this conversation at Dillon's house or his own house. Somewhere a little more private than Dillon's twenty-fifth-floor office with his administrative assistant sitting just outside the doorway. As it was a modern office building with an open floor plan, there was no privacy.

"I hate open floor plans," Chris mumbled.

"What?"

"Nothing. Keep yelling at me. Quietly."

Chris stood opposite Dillon's desk and kept his voice low. Maybe he should have worn a suit, too. This wasn't *Portlandia* in Dillon's law firm. This was Wall Street on the West Coast. His was the only beard on the entire floor.

"Did I mention the part about my bed in my house yet?" Dillon asked.

"Yeah. Although to be fair, you haven't paid me for the bed yet, so technically the bed's still mine."

"I will cut you a check. Then I'll kill you."

"Fair enough."

Dillon groaned and ran his hands through his hair. Funny how nothing changed even as everything changed. In high school, Dillon had been homecoming king their junior year before he got outed. He looked like a Backstreet Boy then and now. Although he'd lived in Portland all his life, Dillon wasn't about to turn into a lumbersexual just because it was the fad. No flannel—silk ties and suits for him. No man bun—he'd rather die. No beard—why hide such a handsome face behind so much hair? Since high school the only thing that had changed about Dillon was the part in his hair and the balance in his bank account. Corporate law had been as good to Dillon as starting his own contracting company had been good to Chris.

"You know this could ruin everything, right?" Dillon asked. "Joey is not a fan of being manipulated. You sleep with her and then offer her a job working for us? She's going to feel manipulated. I don't blame her."

"It just happened, I swear," Chris said. "I was going

to talk to her about the job and then…things. Things happened."

"Naked things."

"Yep."

"You usually have more self-control than that."

"Not around your sister."

"I wish I hadn't heard that."

"Dillon…did you consider she might want to stay at her old job?" Chris asked, desperate to get off the subject of the naked things he had done to Joey last night.

"I know she wants to stay at her old job. I don't want her to stay at her old job. I want her back here working for Lost Lake Village Rentals."

"I do, too."

"Well, that's probably not going to happen now that you had to go and fuck it up by, you know…fucking."

"So you're not mad I slept with her? You're just mad that by sleeping with her I might have ruined your business plan?" Chris asked.

"She's an adult. I don't care who she sleeps with. I'm not Dad. I'm not her keeper. None of my business. Except now it is literally my business. Joey is the single most perfect person to manage Lost Lake Village Rentals and I need her to do it. I can't trust anybody else with it."

"Nobody else?"

"I looked, I swear. I had interviews with almost fifty candidates. Two of them seemed okay until I looked at their Facebook pages. Why do people even have Facebook when they want to remain employed?"

"I like to post Nirvana vids on my MySpace page."

"MySpace doesn't exist anymore."

"Damn, where are all my vids going, then?"

Dillon walked over to Chris and put his hands on his shoulders. "This company is my baby. You don't trust your baby to a stranger. You trust your baby to someone in your family you know and love and who is a marketing genius."

"I've never met a baby who needed marketing."

"My baby does if it's going to get off the ground."

"You have a weird baby."

Dillon dropped his hands from Chris's shoulders and walked back to his desk. Chris had come straight to Dillon's office first thing this morning. He didn't have to be at Timber Ridge until eleven, and as much as it went against the grain to kiss and tell, he knew he had to in this case. He and Dillon were business partners now. Dillon had sunk his entire life savings and his fiancé's into this dream. Lost Lake Village Rentals didn't exist—yet. But it would in a few months if they could get Joey on board. Ten cabins that ringed the famed Lost Lake on the northwest slope of Mount Hood. Ten cabins for nightly, weekly or monthly rent. Ten barely livable cabins Dillon and Oscar had bought with their nest egg and hired Chris to turn into rustic palaces. And somebody had to manage the cabin complex and somebody had to market them and somebody had to live in one of the cabins year-round to troubleshoot guest issues. And that somebody had to be Joey because only Joey had the marketing expertise, the bookkeeping acumen and the personality to deal with the cabin guests. Chris could handle broken pipes and leaky roofs and turning dumps into dream houses but he was not a people person unless he was sleeping with that person. But Joey… This job was tailor-made for her. If only they could convince her of that.

"Sit." Dillon pointed at the chair across from his desk.

"Are you going to kill me in that chair?" Chris asked.

"Do you think I should?"

"I probably would in your shoes." Chris took a seat and knew it might be his last. Dillon had a nice office— all leather furniture and an ebony-stained floor polished to a high shine. If he was going to die somewhere, he was happy to be dying on nicely maintained white-oak flooring. "In my defense, you told me to woo her. You told me to plant a seed—"

"I meant 'plant a seed so she'll think of moving back to Oregon.' I didn't mean plant a seed in…you know. Her…her lady garden."

"This has officially become the second most awkward conversation of my life."

"What was the first?"

"The one I had with Joey last night after—"

"Conversation over."

"Good. Or not good if you're killing me."

"Not going to kill you. But you are going to fix this."

"How am I supposed to 'fix this'? There's nothing to fix. I'll tell her about the job. She'll say 'yes,' 'no' or 'let me think about it.' And that's it. She's an adult. You can't make her do something she doesn't want to do."

"If she says no because she thinks I'm offering it to her out of pity because of the breakup or you're offering it to her because you slept with her, then I'm not going to be happy."

"That's not much of a threat."

"Do you want me to be unhappy? Do you? Bad enough you broke my heart in high school. You want to do it again?"

"I'm going." Chris stood up.

"You remember when I kissed you at the ski lodge?"

"Nope."

"Me, neither. I chickened out. But I wanted to."

"Was that the night we took 'shrooms on a dare?"

"So you do remember."

"How did we survive our senior year?"

"Sheer dumb luck, man," Dillon said.

Chris stood up, leaned across the desk and slapped Dillon on the arm. "It'll be okay. Even if Joey says no, we'll find someone for the job."

"I know." Dillon nodded. "I just remember how it was, the three of us hanging out at the lake all summer. Those were good days. No jobs. No money. Just all of us being stupid kids and not caring about anything. I want a little of that back, you know?"

"I know. I'd like that, too. Minus the drugs and the no money."

"Right."

"I'm having lunch with Joey. I'll tell her more about the company. If she sounds interested, I'll mention the job."

"I want my sister back from the middle of the ocean."

"Maybe she likes living in Hawaii."

"What does Hawaii have that Oregon doesn't?"

Chris leaned over and glanced out the window.

"The sun."

"Overrated. Now go. Get my sister to move back. Sweet-talk her if you have to. But not that way."

"What way?"

"Whatever way you did last night."

"Actually, she—"

"Don't want to hear it. Just go."

"Going."

Chris started to leave, then he stopped in the doorway of Dillon's office. He turned around, raised a hand
and pointed at Dillon.

"I didn't actually break your heart in high school,
did I?"

"No."

"Okay. Good. I'd feel bad if you were in love or
whatever with me back then and I was that clueless."

"You were my best friend, that was it. I wasn't even
that attracted to you. No offense."

"None taken. I wouldn't have crushed on a slacker
like me in high school, either."

"It wasn't that."

"What was it?"

"Dude," Dillon said as if it were the most obvious
thing in the world. "You wore a chain wallet."

CHRIS DROVE FROM Portland up to Timber Ridge and in
traffic it took an hour and a half. He didn't mind the
drive, although it gave him a little too much free time
to think about last night, about Joey, about what happened after and whatever happened this morning that
made her text him. He hadn't expected the text. Not for
one second. Not after she'd cried after the sex and said
the rebound plan hadn't worked.

But really…had he expected it to work? He'd been
through breakups before. One good night of sex with a
friend or stranger wasn't some kind of silver bullet that
could kill the pain. Joey'd been with this guy for two
years. The only thing that might make her feel better
was if Chris took that silver bullet and shot this Ben
guy with it.

He allowed himself to enjoy that murderous fantasy

before remembering he'd never touched a gun in his life. He was a lover, not a fighter. Although it was tempting to make this Ben guy eat shit over what he'd done to Joey. Who did that? Who lied for two straight years to his own girlfriend? And this wasn't a little white lie like saying he was a high school football star when actually he was second string. No, this fucker had a wife. A real live wife living with him in LA and at no point had he bothered to tell Joey that. That was sociopath behavior, lying like that. And lying for that long. Who did that? And more, who did that to Joey? Joey was the kindest girl he'd ever met in his life. She'd looked out for Dillon like some kind of tiny adorable bodyguard during his senior year when things got so bad. And although she was a freshman when Chris was a senior, Joey always helped him with his English homework because he'd been so fucking terrible at anything that involved writing papers. She hadn't mocked him for it, either, hadn't teased him about his bad grammar and spelling. All she'd said was, "Well, you're so good at math it makes me sick, okay?"

Of course he'd fallen in love with her right then and there. He made her sick, she said, and it was the nicest thing any girl had ever said to him. What straight guy with half a brain wouldn't fall in love with her? And now that he knew what she was like in bed? How giving she was? How passionate? How much fun she was during sex? Oh, my God, he was five minutes away from falling in love with her again.

He yanked that thought back, took the keys out of its hands and called in a designated driver. *Go home, Brain, you're drunk on lust.*

When he pulled in for coffee in Government Camp,

he checked his phone, and found he had a new message from Joey.

I can't get over how beautiful the cabin is now. You're so talented it makes me sick. Sorry. Just had to tell you that.

His heart stole the keys and hopped into his truck, grabbed Joey and started off toward the sunset. Then his heart swerved hard, ran off the road, hit a telephone pole and exploded into a fireball.

Oh, fuck.

7

JOEY DROVE UP to Timber Ridge early. She told herself she wanted to see the famous lodge, see if it had changed any since the last time she'd come here several years ago. That's all. It had nothing to do with being particularly eager to see Chris again or anything. In fact, she didn't want to see him again. Her heart raced and her hands felt a little shaky. These were classic symptoms of terror, yes? Yes, of course. She was scared and fear was bad and since she was scared and fear was bad that meant she wasn't looking forward to seeing Chris again already.

And this was why Joey was a marketing genius—she could sell lies to herself.

Except today she wasn't buying.

Joey wanted to see Chris. She absolutely wanted to see him again. Old friend. Dear friend. New friend. All that. But…

But.

Did she want to see him again…naked?

Well, yes.

Easy question. Easy answer.

Did she think she *should* see him again naked?

Harder question. Harder answer.

Ohh…harder.

Stop it, Joey.

Make decisions with the top half of the body, not the bottom half, she told herself.

But the bottom half was so much more fun…

Joey tried to talk some good sense into herself as she walked through the day lodge. Skiing season wouldn't gear up again for another month or so and the place was eerily quiet. And yet it still bore the distinct and lingering scent of hundreds of teenage snowboarders. The ghosts of winters' past, both bitchin' and gnarly. Chris and Dillon were two of those ghosts. Both of them had embraced snowboarding hard their last two years of high school. She'd stuck to regular old-fashioned skis, which actually made sense to her. Plus the snowboarder guys were way too competitive, too intense for her. She'd rather have fun with her friends, ski a little, drink hot chocolate in the lodge instead of risking her neck by trying to prove herself to a bunch of guys she didn't even like, the ones who called the female skiers "Snow Bunnies." Well, they were Ski Dicks to her and her friends. Chris and Dillon weren't Ski Dicks. They were the good guys, although they were pretty ridiculous back then. After a good run, they'd rushed into the lodge, red-faced, sweating, laughing, exhausted, and Dillon would launch into high oratory about his day while Chris stood at his side shaking his head and making the occasional interjection into Dillon's passionate recital—

That was a one-eighty, not a three-sixty. Leave the math to me, Dillon.

*No, that was a Saint Bernard, not a bear. Get your
fucking eyes checked.*

*At no point did you remotely resemble Shaun White
in flight, you dipshit.*

This was apparently how male best friends talked to
each other. Joey found it quite adorable, except for the
unbearable body odor the both of them emitted. She
could smell them before she could see them. Thankfully
since high school they'd figured out how to work both
showers and deodorant. Probably didn't hurt that she'd
given them both an Old Spice gift bag for Christmas
that year with a note that said, "Use it, please! For my
sake and the sake of all humanity! PS—Merry Christmas. PPS—Not kidding, you stink."

Joey laughed to herself as she walked from the ski
lodge and toward the hotel. So many good memories. All of her best ones seemed to involve Dillon
and Chris. And her parents, too. They'd semiadopted
Chris during Dillon's senior year. Dillon was a prime
target for bullying and worse, and Chris was a prime
target for suspension or expulsion what with his ten-
dency to throw punches when confronted by Dillon's
tormentors. Her parents wanted to keep an eye on "the
boys" as they were always called. Chris slept at their
house, ate their food and came with them on all family
trips. He'd fit in so well she hadn't realized how much
a part of her everyday life Chris was until he'd graduated high school. Dillon went to college in New York.
And Chris just…disappeared.

Now she knew where he'd gone. Without Dillon
and her family around, he'd drifted. He'd failed a little
and then succeeded a little and then succeeded a lot.
And all on his own.

And here he was, at age twenty-eight, working at Timber Ridge, which was a National Historic Landmark. How cool was that? She'd had to hire a handyman just to hang the pictures in her Honolulu apartment because she'd been so afraid of damaging the plaster or missing the stud.

Speaking of studs.

At the front desk, Joey asked where she could find Chris. Luckily he'd left word that someone might come looking for him. She skipped the slow and ancient elevator that she guessed still worked at the same speed it had when the place opened eighty years ago and instead took the three flights of steps up to the hotel room. Someone had left the door cracked open but yellow caution tape strung across the frame stopped her in her tracks. A sign on the door apologized for the noise. Noise? What noise?

Joey pushed the door open a few inches, stuck her head inside over the caution tape and saw Chris standing in front of a stone fireplace with a sledgehammer in his hands. He wore safety goggles, knee and elbow pads and a dust mask. He lifted the sledgehammer, turned and swung it hard. The impact was ear-shattering as well as rock-shattering. She jumped, gasped. The fireplace crumbled in a gray waterfall of fractured rock and powder.

"Wow," Joey said, and Chris looked over his shoulder. He pushed the dust mask on top of his head and smiled.

"There's a word for when you do something violent to make yourself feel better," Chris said. "Starts with a *C*? Something Greek or Latin?"

"Catharsis?"

"That's the word."

"You needed catharsis?"

"Kind of, yeah."

Yeah, she kind of knew why he needed catharsis. Oops.

"So...do you feel better now?" she asked. He walked over to her and removed the caution tape to let her inside the room. He shut the door behind them.

"Much."

"Can I try it?"

"Are you bonded, licensed and insured?"

"I have health insurance."

Chris shook his head. "That doesn't count."

"Fine. I'll leave the hammering to you."

"Good."

"That wasn't a sex joke."

"It should have been."

Joey nodded as she looked around the room. "Probably was, now that I think about it. Pretty room. Why are you sledgehammering the fireplace?"

"Mortar cracked a few years ago. Somebody patched it, but they didn't use refractory mortar like you're supposed to. So it's cracking again. Only thing to do is tear it all out and start over."

"Looks messy."

"Gotta make a mess to clean up a mess sometimes."

"There's a metaphor for life in there," she said. "My life, probably."

She went to the king-size bed, pulled back the drop-cloth, and ran her hand over the soft woven covers. Big room. And yet because of all the fir paneling and cedar ceiling beams, it managed to feel cozy and intimate.

Almost romantic. Apart from the huge gaping hole in the fireplace mantel.

"Rough day?" Chris put the head of the sledgehammer on the floor by his foot and he leaned on the handle like a cane.

"Better day actually. I think. Maybe I was too hasty last night when I said, you know…the plan didn't work."

"You just broke up with the guy. You're allowed more than a couple days to get over it. A whole week at least."

She smiled at him, grateful for his understanding.

"Six months. Kira ordered me to not do anything drastic for six months after the breakup."

"What does she consider drastic?"

"Cut my hair off. Get a tattoo. Buy a new car I don't need. Kill someone. Join CrossFit."

"Was that list in order of how drastic they are from least to most?"

"Yeah, pretty much."

"Sounds about right. Six months is fair. After my last breakup I nearly bought a motorcycle to feel better. I don't even know how to ride one."

"Why did you want one, then?"

"Binge-watched *Sons of Anarchy* on Netflix. I wasn't in a good headspace so… I know the feeling. It's okay to take a little time out."

"Speaking of time. About last night… As soon as the shock wore off, and maybe the afterglow, it hit me that I'd spent two years of my life with someone who lied to my face every time we were together. I wasn't crying because I miss him or I want him back. The Ben I thought I loved doesn't exist. I was crying because, well, I didn't have a sledgehammer at the time or anything to hit."

He looked her. Then he looked out the window. Then he looked at the door.

"Chris?"

He walked to the door and locked it before facing her.

"One," he said.

"One what?"

"You get one. And don't tell anyone on earth I let you do this."

He hefted the sledgehammer and held it out to her.

"You're serious?"

"Just one. And be careful. Dillon's already threatened to kill me once today. If you get hurt…"

"I won't get hurt."

She took the sledgehammer from him with both hands. When she felt its incredible weight she had even more respect for Chris. This thing was seriously heavy. She had to set it back down on the ground again.

"Here." Chris put his safety goggles on over her eyes and she adjusted them while he found her a dust mask of her own.

"Okay, any tips?"

"You're right-handed?"

"Yup."

"Grip it so your left hand is at the bottom. Right hand near the head."

Joey placed her hands on the handle just so.

"Hold it tight," Chris said. "Firm grip."

"Got it."

"Now run your right hand down and up the handle again."

"Chris."

"Squeeze it a little. Stroke it. Take your time and

make friends with it. Maybe put a little lube on it. Or lick it. That helps."

"Chris."

"What?"

"I'm going to swing the thing now."

"Swing away."

He took a few steps back, then a few more steps back.

Joey lifted the sledgehammer and held it a moment as she shifted back and forth, trying to find the best angle, the best footing, the best grip. Chris said only one so she had to make this one count. While Joey wasn't a violent person or a particularly angry person, she did wish sometimes she could take a sledgehammer to all the dishonesty, cruelty and wanton stupidity in the world—especially her own. When she lifted the sledgehammer, she didn't pretend the stone fireplace was Ben's face. She just pretended it was her life. And like Chris said, she had to make a mess to clean up a mess.

With her back taut, her stomach sucked in and her shoulders squared, Joey hoisted the sledgehammer, took aim and swung it with all her might. She made contact with the edge of the stone mantel and felt a vibration from her hands all the way to her shoulders. The noise was brief and horrible and yet oddly satisfying, especially as more rock crumbled to the tarp on the floor.

She turned around at the sound of Chris slow-clapping.

"Good job," he said. "I hope you weren't pretending that rock was me."

"Never." She handed him the glasses and the mask. The sledgehammer she laid down onto the floor. "Just… my current disaster zone of a life."

"Feel better?"

"A little bit actually. Thanks."

"No problem. I think we did enough damage to it with the big guns."

"What now?"

"Crowbar."

He dug through his toolbox and pulled out a large iron bar.

"That looks even more fun," she said.

"No."

"Spoilsport."

"This part is easier to mess up."

"I don't want to mess up the fireplace," she said.

"Me, neither. I love this place." Chris glanced around the room. "People come from everywhere to stay at this hotel. They should get a nice fireplace for their money. It's cool to think about, you know."

"What is?"

"Making the fireplace as nice as possible for the people who'll stay here. I won't even be here, but they'll be enjoying my work."

"A big stone fireplace is pretty romantic," she said. "How many people do you think have had great sex in this room?"

"Not enough," he said, and turned his back to her to work. But she could see he was smiling a little. She liked that smile, liked that she could make him smile. Given the chance, she would make him smile again. Maybe this was her chance.

While he worked she watched. With the claw end of the crowbar he pried the gray bricks off the wall. They tumbled onto the tarp leaving bare wood and plaster behind. Chris worked quickly and efficiently. He seemed to be completely untroubled by having her as an audience. If she were him, she wouldn't mind, either. If she could do stuff like this, like rebuilding a fireplace from the floor up, she would want everyone she knew to watch. He didn't seem arrogant about his work, only happy to have the work and determined to do it well. She liked people who could fix things, build things, create things.

Her job entailed coming up with advertising campaigns, reaching out to customers any way she could and building the brand name of Oahu Air. An important job, it helped the company stay in the black and attract new clients. But she never forgot that the entire company wouldn't exist but for the men and women who built the airplanes and the airport workers who kept them clean, safe and airworthy. As much as she liked her job, she wished she was doing something that spoke to her heart a little more than coming up with new headers for the company newsletter or spending a solid week picking a font for a new advertising poster. She wished she could do something that made her feel like Chris did when he worked, like he was making the world a little nicer, a little more comfortable and romantic for people. Preferably a job that didn't involve so much sweating, however. Sweat looked much better on Chris than it did on her.

He finished dismantling the entire fireplace in about half an hour. She offered to help him load the old firebricks into the wheelbarrow but he waved her aside.

"Man's work?" she teased.

"It is," he said. "If that man is licensed, bonded and insured."

"Fine, fine. I'll just go get us a table for lunch. We're still having lunch, right?" she asked.

He glanced over her shoulder at the bedside clock.

"It's still a little early. You hungry?"

"I didn't come early for lunch. I came… I don't know," she admitted. "I sort of wanted to see you. I also sort of wanted to not ever see you again because I felt like such an asshole last night. But then I sort of wanted to see you because I was such an asshole last night. I'm very conflicted."

"I can tell."

"Do you mind?"

"That you're conflicted?"

"Yeah."

"No. But why are you so conflicted? It's just me," Chris said.

"It's not just you."

"We've known each other forever."

"We haven't seen each other since high school."

"Yeah, but still. We're old friends."

"Old friends. Old buddies. Old pals. Who fucked last night. Hard."

"Would it have made it less weird if we'd fucked soft?"

"Less weird, maybe, but also less fun."

"You liked it." Chris narrowed his eyes at her.

"You know I did."

"How much did you like it?"

He moved in closer to her.

"Now don't do that," she said. "I already feel kind of bad for using you as my rebound guy. Don't force me to reuse you."

"What if I want to be reused?"

"Do you?"

"Who wouldn't?"

"Chris, I'm being serious." She plopped down on

the bed and grabbed a pillow to cling to. He crossed his arms over his chest and looked down at her. With the slight gray dust from the demolished fireplace in his hair and his flannel shirt rolled up to his elbows, he looked very manly. And handsome. And sexy. And a lot of other things she shouldn't think about while trying not to have sex with him.

"Tell me what's happening in your brain right now," he said. His voice was calm as was his demeanor. No pressure. Just curiosity.

"Tug-of-war."

"Tell me more."

"I'm worried about being a bad person," she said.

"You aren't a bad person. You've never been a bad person. You couldn't be a bad person if you tried, although…" He paused and raised one finger. "I might like to see you try."

She rolled her eyes at him.

"A bad person uses people for their own ends, right?" she asked.

"I'm being used today."

"By me?"

"By the hotel. They hired me to do a job. They are using me."

"They are paying you."

"Payment comes in many forms."

"Well, I care about you. You know, since we're old buddies."

"Old pals."

"Old friends."

"We're really not that old," Chris said.

"True. But we are friends, right?"

He nodded.

"I go back to Hawaii on November 1, the day after Dillon's wedding. I don't want to spend the next two weeks having sex with you just to leave you and hurt you. And I realize I'm projecting because I know if I spent the next two weeks having sex with you and then went back to work, it would hurt me."

"It's only eleven days until you leave."

"Oh, you know what I mean."

"I know. But I also know a lot of things hurt."

"That's your answer?"

"It's true. A lot of stuff in life hurts. And not all of it's bad. Didn't your arms hurt when you hammered that mantel?"

"Yeah. Felt it all the way down my back."

"But you liked it?"

"Kind of. Is that weird?"

"Do you work out?"

"I run."

"Does it hurt?"

"Sometimes."

"Do you quit because it hurts?"

"Not unless I'm injured."

"So just because something hurts doesn't mean you shouldn't do it. Right?"

"Are you trying to get me into bed?"

"Well…you're already on the bed. Into bed seems like the next logical step."

"Did you put a condom back in your toolbox?"

"No."

"No?"

"I put ten in it."

Joey's eyes widened.

"You know, just in case you wanted…"

"I want."

He took a step forward.

She held up her hand. He stopped.

"I want," she repeated. "But."

"But?"

But.

There were a lot of buts.

But she had a job in Hawaii she'd be going back to soon.

But she didn't want to hurt his feelings by fucking him and dumping him.

But she really didn't want to get hurt again herself so closely after enduring the worst breakup of her life.

But her life was at a crossroads right now and complicating it by getting into a short-term relationship with someone wouldn't make things any easier.

And yet.

"Spicy Indian food," she said.

"What about it?"

"I love it. Absolutely love it. And I always eat too much of it when I go to an Indian restaurant and I'm always miserable after. But I never regret eating it."

"Did you just compare sleeping with me to eating Indian food?"

"You said it was okay to do stuff that hurts sometimes. Eating spicy curry does that."

"You're a little weird, Jo."

"You compared fucking me to being an astronaut last night."

"I didn't say I wasn't weird, too. Also I'm going to have sex with you right now."

"No, you aren't. We need to talk about this a little bit more."

"I'm hard already. Just FYI. No pressure."

"It'll be a short talk. You have to make me a promise. And you can't break this promise."

"What's the promise?"

"You have to promise me you won't try to make me stay. You won't try to make us more than just a two-week thing. You won't force me to make a big drastic decision about the future when I can barely figure out today, okay? If last night is any indicator of how we are together, the next couple of weeks will be fun."

"Understatement, but I'm with you so far."

"It'll be fun and we'll be all horny for each other and me leaving to go back to work will suck. But you have to swear you won't mess with my head or try to talk me out of it or anything. This breakup with Ben has been hellish, okay? I can't jump into another serious relationship for a while. I need that six months at least. If we're going to do this—"

"We are."

"I need you to work with me and not against me. If you can swear you won't make leaving more difficult than it's going to be in two weeks, then I'm in."

"I can do that. I can make that promise."

"Is that your conscience talking or your, you know, sledgehammer?"

"Can't tell. They have the same voice, oddly enough. Gets really confusing."

"Chris."

"Okay, okay," Chris said. He kicked open his toolbox and dug around in the bottom. "Here it is."

He stood up and held something in his hand. Not a tool. Not a box of condoms. It looked like…

"Is that a CD?" she asked.

"It is."

"I'd forgotten what they looked like."

"It's not just any CD, by the way. This is *In Utero*, Nirvana's best album, their last album, and it is signed by Dave Grohl. I waited in the rain for five hours to get this CD signed. I listen to it in its entirety at least once a week."

"Are you going to listen to it…now?" she asked, deeply and profoundly confused by what Nirvana had to do with this current discussion.

"Not unless you want really creepy mood music for the sex. I'm going to swear on it. It will make the promise legally binding. To me, anyway. So you hold it."

She took the CD from him feeling both moved and amused by his sincerity.

Chris placed his right hand on the CD and raised his left hand.

"Go on," he said. "I'll make the oath."

"Do you solemnly swear that you will not try to stop me from returning to Hawaii on November 1?"

"I solemnly swear that I will not attempt to stop you from returning to Hawaii on November 1. Wait. What day of the week is that?"

"Sunday."

"Then I definitely won't stop you from going back. That's football day."

"Good. Go Seahawks. One more—do you solemnly swear you won't make it harder for me to leave than it's already going to be?"

"I solemnly swear I won't make it harder for you to leave than it's already going to be."

"Do you swear on this signed copy of *In Utero* that you, Chris Steffensen, will not make it weird for us?"

"I solemnly swear that I will not make it weird—except in the good way. Now can I please put my cock inside any and every part of you that you will allow me to get inside?"

"Yes. But no butt stuff today. I'm still jet-lagged."

"I have no idea what jet lag has to do with your asshole and—I'll be honest—I don't want to know."

"You really don't."

"Sex now?"

"Can I be on top this time?"

"If you insist," he said with a put-upon sigh. Despite the sigh she saw the twinkle of amusement in his eyes.

"Should we, uh, get a room?"

"We have a room. I'm working alone."

"You won't get in trouble?"

"I don't charge by the hour. Plus I'm actually staying here tonight while I work. Easier than commuting from Portland every day."

"So we'll make this your lunch break, right?"

"Right," he said. "My favorite meal of the day."

8

JOEY CUPPED THE side of his face to deepen the kiss. He moved forward, rolling her onto her back.

"So we're really doing this?" she asked as he rubbed her breasts over her shirt. "We're going to sleep together until I go back to Hawaii?"

"I would like that."

He said it so simply, those four words. *I would like that.* But she heard more than the words in his tone. She heard longing, a lovely sound. He wanted her. How nice of him. No denying she wanted him, too. How could she not? She had eyes to see his handsome face and ears to hear the warm masculine timbre of his voice when he spoke. She had a nose to smell the clean scent of his boring guy soap and hands to feel the strength of his body as she touched him and held him. And she had lips and a tongue to taste him. Delicious, yes. That was the word for him. She'd be a glutton in the next weeks, trying to get her fill of him before leaving. And yes, it would hurt when she went back to Hawaii but it would be a better pain because it was an honest pain. They'd talked about it, consented to it, agreed to take on the pain together. And it was a pain she'd chosen, not the kind of pain Ben had forced on her with his lies. A good pain. The sort of pain one earns and feels a little proud of. She'd have sex with this beautiful man until she left, and in compensation for the pain of leaving him, she would take two weeks of beautiful memories with her of a man who helped her trade a bad pain for a good pain.

Chris slipped a hand under her shirt and she arched her back to let him unhook her bra. As soon as he did he pushed her shirt and bra up together and licked her nipples one at a time. They hardened against his hot tongue and inside his mouth. She breathed heavily but softly, aware that people might be in the rooms on either side. Hammering and drilling were normal sounds to come from a room under construction, not moaning and groaning. As Chris sucked her breasts, she went to work on his buttons, opening them quickly, eager to undress him.

When she was a kid, she'd had romantic fantasies about this hotel. How could she not with all the cute teenage snowboarders running around the place and the older men in their twenties and thirties with their skis and their beautiful girlfriends in designer ski gear. She'd wanted to be one of those girlfriends in her white boots and white snow pants, white jacket and blond hair in perfect twin braids peaking out from under a white hat. They'd come into the lodge together, rosy cheeked from exertion, laughing and sweaty, looking like the very picture of luxurious adulthood. And those couples got to stay in the big rooms at Timber Ridge, the ones with king-size beds and stone fireplaces with turn-down service and bottles of wine and no adult supervision because they were adults and could do anything they wanted alone in hotel rooms.

Even sex.

Joey ached to be an adult back in high school, ached to be one of those beautiful pampered girlfriends. The thought of getting a hotel room in a ski lodge with a hot guy and being old enough that no one could tell them what to do in that hotel room had been the number-one dream of her entire freshman year of high school. And now it was coming true.

If only for a couple weeks.

If only.

Nothing to do but enjoy it while it lasted.

In her teenage fantasies, she hadn't imagined sleeping with the guy who actually worked at the hotel but her teenage fantasies were pretty vague on where the money for the expensive room came from. A real man with gainful employment was much sexier than a fantasy dude who might be hiding massive credit card debt.

Joey ran her fingers through Chris's hair as he kissed her nipples. She laughed as a chunk of fireplace mortar came out in her hand.

"What?" He raised his head to meet her eyes.

"I found something." She held out the chunk. He shook his head and dust flew off his hair.

"I should take a shower."

"I like how dirty you are."

He raised his eyebrow.

"Do you?"

"Very much so."

"You know, I usually don't do what I did last night," he said, and for a second he looked almost embarrassed, adorably embarrassed.

"Do what? Have great sex?"

"No, I do that whenever I can. But…I was a little more real with you than I usually am the first time I sleep with somebody."

"You mean like when you held me down by my wrists and you whipped your cock out and told me to suck it and all that?"

"That's kind of what I mean, yeah. I usually hold off on that for a while. If it was too much I can tone it down."

"Why didn't you hold off on it with me?"

"I don't know. I guess I just felt comfortable with you. But if it made you uncomfortable—"

"It didn't."

"No?"

"I liked seeing that side of you. I thought you were so quiet and laid-back."

"I am."

"Not last night. You were intense last night."

"Too intense?"

"Perfect," she said, wrapping her arms around his neck to pull him closer. She needed to get him naked and fast. Her body remembered the warmth of his skin on hers and ached to feel it again. "I want you to be with me the way you want to be with me. Don't hold back. I can take it."

"You took it last night pretty well."

"Only pretty well?"

"Very well," he said, nuzzling his lips to her neck. "You want to take it again?"

"And again and again and again…"

Chris kissed her mouth and she ran her hands down his back. She slipped her hands under his shirt, desperate to touch him. After all that hard work, his body had grown hot to the touch and her cool skin bristled with pleasure as his heat suffused her. She wanted more more more of him and she couldn't get it fast enough.

"Please get naked," she said into his ear as his fingers found her jeans zipper.

"You first."

"But—"

"Wait. Patience is its own reward."

"So is your body."

"If you don't behave…"

She heard the warning tone in his voice and she liked it way too much.

"If I don't behave, then what?" she asked.

"I don't know," he said as he knelt and started pulling her jeans down. "But I know we'll both like it."

He had her naked in seconds but he kept his clothes on. She found this both delightful and infuriating. And she told him so.

"You're greedy," he said as he nudged her legs open with his knees.

"I'm wet."

"You're trying to get me naked before I'm ready. It won't work."

"I'm really, really wet?"

"I'll take my clothes off when I'm good and ready and not a second sooner."

"You're doing this to torture me."

"I might be. But this should make up for it."

"What will make—"

Chris slipped a finger inside her.

"Oh, that," she said. "That's a start."

"You weren't lying. You are wet."

He lay on his side and cradled her head in his arm and against his chest as he touched her. This was unexpectedly pleasant—naked skin against his flannel. His shirt felt as soft and warm as the sheets she'd slept on as a kid at the cabin. If Chris wasn't careful she would steal one of his flannel shirts to take back with her to Hawaii.

Joey closed her eyes and moved her hips with his hand as Chris stroked inside her, first with one finger, then two and finally three. The man was good with his hands, that was for sure. He was gentle and slow. No pistoning, no prodding. Just caressing, exploring, stimulating.

"What feels good to you?" he said into her ear, and if she hadn't been wet before, that question asked by this man in that tone of voice would do it.

"Um, well, if you push in a little a few inches inside and rub back and forth that's good."

"Here?" He touched a spot.

"A little higher."

"Here?"

He touched another spot and Joey inhaled sharply.

"Yeah," Chris said. "That was it."

"That was it," she said breathlessly.

He pushed into the spot, softly at first and then harder. She could sense him watching her face, listening to her breathing, gauging her reactions.

"Can you come from this?" he asked as he rubbed that spot inside her in a tight circle.

"If you keep doing that I will."

"Then I will keep doing this. I want to feel you come on my fingers."

"Then will you get naked?"

"If you come on my fingers?"

"Yes."

"Absolutely," he said. "But I better feel it."

"Keep doing that and you'll feel it."

"I won't stop until you beg me to. And only then."

He kissed her ear and she shivered at his warm mouth and hot breath on his skin. Shivered again as he massaged inside her. And God, it was good. His fingers grazed every nerve along the wet inner walls of her body. Pleasure spiked deep into her stomach, up her back, into her upper thighs. Her head fell back and she moaned quietly.

"You can be louder," Chris said.

"I don't want the neighbors to hear."

"They've put up with me sledgehammering today. Trust me, the sound of you coming is much better than that."

"Maybe I don't want them to hear me come. Maybe I only want you to hear me come." She met his eyes and smiled. He kissed that smile right off her face. And still his fingers moved in her as he kissed her. In all her life she'd never had a more wicked, teasing man inside her. He seemed to know just when she was getting this close to coming. Then he'd push in deeper or turn his hand or pause to kiss her breasts again. Anything to delay her orgasm. Yet she couldn't complain. Who would? An incredibly sexy man had his fingers inside her. This was so much better than lunch.

"Please let me come," she said.

"Why do you want to come so much?" he asked, brushing her clitoris lightly with his thumb. "Aren't you enjoying this?"

"I love it."

"Then I shouldn't rush."

"But you won't get naked until I come."

"No, ma'am. I won't."

"I want you naked and I want to come and you won't let me. So unfair."

"Caught between a cock and a hard place, aren't you? You poor thing."

Joey laughed, which should have been an awkward thing, laughing while completely naked with three fingers that weren't hers inside her. But it didn't feel awkward. It felt right. Everything with Chris felt right. Too right. She would steal more than his flannel shirts to take back with her when she returned home to Hawaii. If he wasn't careful, she'd steal him, too.

"Chris." She looked him straight in the eyes.

"Joey."

"I would rather have you naked right now than come, that's how bad I want you naked. And that's bad. Because I really want to come."

She tensed her inner muscles around his fingers so he knew she meant it.

"Damn," he said. "You trying to break my hand?"

"Never. I like those hands too much."

"They like you. They like you very, very much."

"If they really liked me, they would strip your clothes off you. That's what hands are good for."

"How about we make a deal?"

"I like your deals."

"I let you come now. And then I take off my clothes. And you let me come on you."

"On me?"

He nodded. "On you."

"Deal," she said. "Should we shake on it?"

"Well. I would. But…" He glanced down at his hand

between her thighs. "Let's just call it an oral agreement. No, that's a different thing."

"You're wonderful," she said because she couldn't help herself, because he was wonderful. He was, in fact, every kind of wonderful she could think of—sexy, sweet, totally wicked in bed, handsome, talented, hard-working, hard. Very, very hard.

Chris's expression changed a little when she said that. He didn't smile like she thought he would. The look he gave her was almost somber, a little wistful.

"What?" she asked.

"Nothing. Just trying to remember what I told you about good pain."

"Hurts already," she said.

"But still worth it."

"Definitely still worth it."

They kissed once more, a long, lingering kiss. She would think about this kiss and this moment when she was on the plane back to Hawaii. She knew that already. And she would remind herself what they decided, that they were adults who were allowed to make choices they would later regret. Or not regret.

But probably regret.

But Joey didn't regret it yet. So she threw her leg over Chris's to open up more for him, to invite him deeper and to take what he had to give her for as long as they had together.

Inside her she felt the sweetest ache and his fingers rubbed that ache. The miracle of his touch was that the ache grew stronger the more he touched it, and yet only his touch could relieve the aching. He caused the ache. He cured the ache. He made her ache all over again.

Joey clung to his shoulder as he touched her, and

it wasn't long before she was there, right there, at the edge again so ready to come she could scream. But she didn't want to scream because she'd told Chris the truth—she wanted only him to hear her come. Her pleasure was for his ears only. She breathed heavy and hard as muscles inside her knitted themselves into taut knots that clenched and released, clenched and released, and clenched and held and clenched, and tightened... and then released all at once, all around his fingers, all around his hand.

With a soft moan Joey's head fell back onto the bed and her entire body went soft and slack. She heard Chris chuckling, a sexier sound she'd rarely heard.

"Good girl. You almost broke my hand."

"I'd apologize but...I don't want to."

"No apologies necessary."

"Your turn," she said.

"It is, isn't it."

Chris slid off the bed and stood up. Somehow Joey found the strength to lift her head and watched him undress. He kept his promise and stripped completely naked for her. She liked the way he took his clothes off—so perfunctory, so careless. He wasn't putting on a show for her. Just getting the job done. When he shed his boxer briefs she saw his erection, already hard and thick and eager for her. And she wanted it inside as much as it wanted to be in her. He rolled on a condom and settled in on top of her. There it was, the heat of his naked skin on hers again, that delicious heat. She craved it and her skin tingled with happiness to feel his weight and his length and his hardness against her from shoulder to thigh.

"You still want to be on top?" he asked.

She nodded. "If you'll let me."

"For a few minutes. But only because you said please and only because I'm such a gentleman."

He wrapped his arms around her and rolled them so that he lay on his back and she on top of him. Now that she'd come she was both wet and open. She grasped his cock in her hand, guided him inside her and slid back to take every inch. Chris inhaled as she enveloped him with her body and his eyes closed and she was pretty sure she'd never forget this moment as long as she lived. Carefully she moved on him, finding a pace and a rhythm that suited them both. She placed her hands flat on his chest to hold herself over him and moved her hips in a slow undulation that took him deep within her and then out nearly to the tip before taking him back in again. Chris ran his calloused fingertips up her bare back and she sighed and giggled at the tickling sensation. Her nipples hardened from the gentle pressure of his hands on her.

"I only get eleven days with you." She sighed. "I want you in every way. On top. On bottom. From behind. Against the wall."

"Flat on your back on the bench seat in my pickup with your skirt yanked up around your waist and your ass in my hands?"

"You've given this some thought."

"That might be a leftover fantasy from high school."

"Truck sex?"

"Truck sex."

"You bring the truck. I'll bring the skirt."

"Another deal," he said.

He took her hips in his hands to guide her movements. Even underneath her he still had to be in charge.

She didn't mind letting someone else run the show if that person knew exactly what he was doing. Which Chris did. God, did he know what he was doing. Under her he rocked his hips back and forth while he guided her up and down the length of him. Joey groaned and dropped her head to his chest, kissing it, biting it, biting his collarbone and shoulders, as he rocked more and more beneath her. The temperature in the room skyrocketed. Chris kissed her neck—hard. And sucked her nipples—hard. And when it seemed he couldn't stand being trapped on the bottom anymore, he rolled them onto her back and thrust into her—hard.

Joey didn't complain about the sudden change of position. She had nothing to complain about, and even if she wanted to complain, she was too busy panting to get any words out. Chris rode her with long deep thrusts and his strong hands on her ribs right under her breasts, holding her down gently but firmly, putting her in her place, which was under him and around him and with him, and that was a damn good place to be in that moment.

She loved the way he fucked her so that she felt sexy and dirty and wicked and yet somehow safe and comfortable, too. She couldn't stop touching him now, running her hands up his taut arms to his broad shoulders and down his chest and his stomach to his hips and iron thighs that he used to control his powerful thrusts. She felt him lifting her off the bed and knew he wasn't and yet with her eyes closed it seemed she floated with him a few inches up and going higher, and higher, still higher…and with a crash she came down again as she shook with an orgasm she hadn't expected so quickly after her first one. As she came back to awareness, she felt warm wetness on her stomach and breasts. She opened her eyes to see Chris holding his cock in his hands, coming on her body in a few hard spurts. She met his eyes—they were open—and she didn't look away. It was terrifyingly intimate, locking eyes as he came. He looked at her with real desire, real tenderness. Honest desire. Honest tenderness. There was no deceit in Chris Steffensen. None. What she saw was what she got and what she saw was pretty damn good.

Chris exhaled heavily and she watched the last of his tension drain from his body. He bent and kissed her lightly on the lips.

"I liked that," he whispered.

"Me, too," she whispered back. They had no reason to whisper other than lovers whispered in bed and they were officially lovers now.

"Take a shower with me."

"Is that an order?"

"If you obey it, it is."

"Then it's an order."

He grabbed her by the wrist and pulled her off the bed. The bathroom was lovely, if rustic, or perhaps lovely *and* rustic. She wondered if the tile on the floor was original to the hotel.

"I don't know," Chris said. "They're good at finding craftsmen who can match the original look."

"Like you?"

"The fireplace is easy work. The sons and grand-sons of the original carpenters do most of the heavy lifting around here." Chris turned on the shower and the water heated up quickly. "I was here one day with them and this old guy and his wife walked past us. He slapped his hand down on a beam and said, 'Now this is good old-fashioned craftsmanship. They sure don't build stuff like they used to.' The carpenter next to me leaned and in said, 'Let's not tell him I replaced that beam last week.'"

Joey laughed as she stepped into the shower, doing her best to keep her hair out of the stream of water. She didn't need to rewash her hair. Thankfully Chris had good aim—in several ways. He went completely under the water, however, and with her hands full of shampoo she scrubbed every particle of stone and old fireplace dust out of his near-blond hair. Then he returned the favor but soaping up his hands and washing his semen off her stomach and breasts. It didn't take long but he seemed to linger over the work.

Chris held her by the waist and kissed her under the hot water. She saw him looking down at her wet body and shaking his head.

"What?" she asked.

"I was just thinking that you are definitely worth the trouble."

"Am I trouble?"

"Not really. Just…Dillon's going to kill me. He told me that this morning."

"Why does Dillon even care? He's getting married in ten days—on my birthday, let me remind you. I should be killing *him*."

"He's going to kill me because I was supposed to talk to you about something and I didn't talk to you about it because, you know…"

"We had sex instead."

"It seemed like the right thing to do at the time."

"What's the thing you're supposed to talk about?"

"Doesn't matter."

"It does matter."

"Okay, it does," Chris said. "But I can't tell you."

"Why not?"

"Because I promised I wouldn't try to make you stay."

"Stay where?"

"Stay in Oregon at Lost Lake."

"Why should I stay at Lost Lake? I have a job, you know, and it's not in Lost Lake."

"He wants to hire you for a job."

"Dillon wants to hire me? I'm not a lawyer."

"Not at his law firm. At Lost Lake Village Rentals."

"Never heard of it."

"It doesn't exist—yet. Dillon and Oscar bought a bunch of houses out at Lost Lake, old cabins, and they hired me to fix them up. We're going to rent them out."

"We?"

"I'm an investor, too."

"Interesting," she said. "So what's the situation?"

"Eight out of ten cabins are now in good shape. The other two will be done by spring. Since now's about when people start getting sick of the weather and start booking their summer vacations, we need a property manager who's also good at marketing, who knows the vacation market and who can run a website and deal with people. We need someone we can trust. So…you basically."

"So Dillon's going to kill you because you fucked me instead of offering me a job?"

"Right. I was supposed to talk to you about it. I didn't do that. Now Dillon's pissed at me because he thinks you won't take the job because we're sleeping together. You and me, not me and Dillon."

"That's ridiculous. I wouldn't turn down the job just because you and I are sleeping together," she said. "And I'm truly flattered that you both think so highly of my skills."

"So you'll take the job?"

Joey laughed and kissed him. He was so cute with water dripping off his hair and beard she couldn't help herself.

"Absolutely not."

"Worth a shot. But we can keep fucking, right?"

"Absolutely yes."

9

JOEY HAD HER first sex regret with Chris later that evening while driving to dinner. She regretted not eating something after all the sex she'd had with Chris that afternoon. Nearly seven o'clock and her stomach felt like it was trying to eat itself she was so hungry. Next time she would plan things out better. In the future when picking sex over food, they would take the time to eat after. Had to keep up their strength, after all.

Dillon had asked her to meet him and Oscar at a brewery near his office that evening and she hoped and prayed that it was one of those micro brewpubs that also served food. Lots and lots of food. When she arrived, Dillon and Oscar had already gotten a table. They waved her over and Dillon stood up and embraced her.

"Welcome home," her big brother said as she fell into the comfort of his arms. "You've been gone too long and I hate you." He felt the same—annoyingly taller than she was. And smelled the same—way too expensive cologne. But the smile on his face was different than the old tight, stressed-out fake smile he used to wear. Tonight's smile was broad, genuine, happy. And she had a feeling it was all thanks to the man sitting at the table next to him.

"Hawaii is as close to Portland as Portland is to Hawaii," she said as she pulled out of the hug to smile up at him. "And I hate you, too. Can I meet your fiancé now as I already like him better than you?"

"Jo, this is Oscar, the love of my life until he gets old and wrinkly. Oscar, Joey, my sister, who is currently the bane of my existence. Which is only fair as I was hers for a couple years."

"Twenty-five years," she said. "Hi, Oscar. You are way more handsome than Dillon. Are you sure you don't want to hold out for someone hotter?"

"I heard his sister was taken," Oscar said as he stood up and dropped his napkin neatly on the table. She couldn't fault her brother for falling for Oscar. He was over six feet tall, dark-skinned, dark-eyed and wore a suit better than James Bond. "So second best, it is."

"Oh, I like him," she said.

"Hands off," Dillon said. "I mean, after you hug him."

"My pleasure." She reached out and hugged her brother's too-elegant fiancé, and the hug he gave her in return felt like family already. "It's so wonderful to meet you finally."

"And you, too." Oscar let her go and they sunk comfortably into their chairs, friends already. "Dillon said the wedding would only officially be on once we met and I had your approval."

"Are you nice to him?" she asked, pointing at Dillon.

"His well-being is my number-one priority," Oscar said.

"What's your number-two priority?" she asked.

"Food."

"Awesome," she said. "Mine, too."

"We both love food and Dillon, and not in that order," Oscar said. "Is the wedding on?"

"You have my blessing." Joey lifted her glass of ice water in a toast.

"Whew," Dillon said. "Thank God. I didn't want to have to ask for our deposit on the ballroom back. Weddings are expensive, Jo. Don't have one."

"Well, you don't have to worry about that," she said with a sigh as she picked up the menu. "I sent Ben packing."

"About time."

She glared at him.

"I mean…sorry." Dillon tried to look sympathetic. He failed but she appreciated that he tried. "I'm sure you…miss…him…maybe?"

Dillon glanced over at Oscar, who hid his eyes behind a menu.

"I know you both know Chris and I are…seeing each other while I'm in town. You don't have to pretend you don't know. And I know he told you I broke up with Ben."

"Not to give you relationship advice you don't want or need…" Dillon began.

"Then don't."

"But."

"I knew that *but* was coming."

Oscar snorted a laugh.

Dillon cleared his throat. "But…a little advice from a man who has had way too many rebound flings."

"How many are we talking?" Oscar asked, his eyes narrowed.

"Hush and read your menu," Dillon said. "But the

thing with rebound guys is…your rebound guy should be someone you'd never have a real relationship with. You save the good ones for real love. Like I did."

"That's better," Oscar said.

"You two are getting married in eleven days. Why are we talking about me and Chris?" she asked. "Can't we talk about you two? Wedding stuff?"

"Boring," Oscar said.

"So boring," Dillon agreed. "At this point we want to talk about anything but the wedding."

"Not even to tell me why you're making all of us dress up? And why you're having the wedding on my birthday? Hmm?" She winked at Dillon so he'd know she was kidding.

"That's my fault." Oscar raised his hand, gave her an appropriately apologetic look. "I told Dillon I'd always wanted a Halloween wedding and he said yes before mentioning that was his sister's birthday."

"I didn't think you'd really mind," Dillon said.

"I'm turning twenty-six, not six. And I can think of no better way to celebrate my birthday than by partying at your wedding. But…"

"But?" Dillon said.

"But I still better get a really good present."

"I knew I should have married the sister," Oscar said. "A woman after my own heart."

Dinner passed quickly in a haze of good conversation, food and seasonal IPAs. She and Dillon ordered pumpkin-flavored beers while Oscar stuck to water and wine. All went well until Dillon asked the one question she didn't want to answer.

"So what happened with you and Ben?"

"We broke up," she said, then took the last bite of her

gluten-free brownie she'd gotten for dessert. She wasn't allergic to gluten but for some reason every single dessert on the menu was gluten-free. No explanation except she was definitely back in Portland.

"Can I ask why?"

"You're being nosy, dear," Oscar said. "If she wants to talk about it, she'll talk about it."

"I really don't want to talk about it," she said.

"Do I need to kill him? Just answer that question." Dillon reached out and grabbed her hand. "I really want to kill someone."

"No one is killing anyone," she said, pointing at him and at Oscar. "I already heard you threatened Chris."

"Why did he threaten to kill Chris?" Oscar asked her. "He's pretty. I won't allow it."

"Ask him." She nodded at Dillon, looking sheepish.

"I love you, man, but if you start killing handsome guys, we're going to have words. There aren't that many of us around," Oscar said.

"I just threatened him a little." Dillon held up his fingers only half an inch apart. "I gave him a job to do and then he screwed up the job."

"He didn't screw up the job. He screwed the sister," Joey said to Oscar.

"That is not true."

"It is true," she said. "I was there. Screwing happened."

"No, I mean, I didn't threaten to kill him because they're a thing. I don't care they're a thing. They can be a thing all they want wherever they want whenever they want in any depraved manner they want. I assume it was depraved? I always got that vibe from Chris."

"Mildly depraved," she said.

"Thought so," Dillon continued. "But…I need her to run Lost Lake and she won't, and that's all Chris's fault."

"Not his fault," she said.

"Really? Then whose fault is it?"

"Nobody's fault," Joey said, sitting back in her chair. The brownie, which had been the size of her head, was now reduced to the size of her hand. She surrendered. But she'd probably take it home with her.

"I refuse to believe that," Dillon said. "Everything is always somebody's fault."

"Then it's my fault." Joey shrugged and sat forward. Maybe she wouldn't surrender to her giant brownie quite yet. "I can't quit my job. It would be like letting Ben win."

"Ah…" Oscar nodded at Dillon. Dillon nodded at Oscar.

"Stop nodding," she said, attacking her brownie with a second wind. "I can see you two nodding."

"So it's Ben's fault?" Oscar asked.

"You might as well tell us," Dillon said. "You're going to tell me eventually, anyway."

"He's married and he didn't tell me."

Dillon stood up. Calmly.

"Where are you going?" she asked.

"Hawaii. I need to kill someone."

"Sit." She grabbed his jacket and pulled down. He sat.

"He was married and didn't tell you?" Oscar sounded horrified. Dillon looked too angry to speak.

"For two years," she said. "Two years we dated. Maybe one year total if you count all those trips he took to LA. He worked in the Oahu and California offices. I thought it was just work stuff taking him back and forth. He's a VP of Operations so it made sense."

"Is that allowed? VPs and marketing managers dating?" Oscar asked. It was a fair question.

"Not technically, but we didn't work together. I have my own boss and didn't answer to Ben for anything. We justified it that way. I didn't think for one second he had a wife back in LA. Until I went to surprise him on the way here. It was bad."

"I can't even imagine." Oscar shook his head. "I'm sorry. Truly."

"Thank you. I appreciate that." She smiled at her brother's future husband and knew Dillon had found one of the good ones. "But that's why I can't take the job. I can't quit now. If I quit, Ben wins. He gets to keep his job and keep his secret and keep doing what he's been doing. At least if I'm there, I can make sure it doesn't happen to someone else. All I have to do is mention 'Ben's wife' at a staff meeting one day and everyone will know."

"Sweet, sweet revenge," Dillon said. Joey rolled her eyes.

"This isn't revenge. He did something horrible to me, and I refuse to walk away and let him win."

"I understand the feeling, Joey," Oscar said, "but you know you can't police the man for the rest of his life. Eventually he'll get another job or you will and he'll lie to as many women as he wants, and there's nothing you can do about it."

"I know. I know." She raised her hands. "But you know Ben is at home right now hoping and praying I'm mad enough to quit work. That's his dream. He knows I can make his life hell when I go back to work. Quit-

ting would be playing into his hands. It's exactly what
he would want. I can't give him what he wants, not after
what he did to me. And his wife, too. God, that poor
woman. I hope she strangles him."

"If she won't, I will," Dillon said.

"No, you won't. You're getting married and you can't
get married in jail," Joey reminded him. "You're going
to focus on Oscar, on the wedding, on finding me the
perfect birthday present to make up for you two stealing my birthday. My favorite color is red. My shoe size
is seven. My ring size is six and a half and diamonds
are a girl's best friend, but emeralds and sapphires are
also on very good terms with most women. And that is
that. No more talk of Ben or Chris or me. Tell me about
the wedding. That's an order."

AFTER DINNER, SHE kissed both Dillon and Oscar goodbye and headed back to her Lost Lake cabin with one-
quarter of a gluten-free brownie tucked in her purse.
She'd save that for later. Later was most likely "as soon
as she got back in the cabin." Her self-control was du-
bious at best and nonexistent where gorgeous men and
chocolate desserts were concerned. She'd even tried to
combine them once and quickly discovered she wasn't
the sort of person who liked to mix her pleasures. Licking chocolate fudge off an erect penis made the fudge
taste weird and the penis unfuckable until after a long
shower. Lesson learned. She wouldn't try that with
Chris. She loved the way he tasted. Not even chocolate could make that man any more delicious than he
already was.

Joey found herself grinning as she unlocked the
cabin and went inside. Four days past a breakup and

already grinning like a fool in lust. Maybe she could talk Chris into coming down to her cabin for a nightcap. Of course the drive was pretty long—about an hour between the lake and Timber Ridge. And it was late. Late-ish, anyway. Ten-ten. By the time he came down to the cabin it would be eleven-thirty probably. Then they'd talk awhile, and fuck awhile, and talk some more. That would take at least an hour and a half. By the time they were done it would be, oh, one in the morning? That was definitely too late for him to drive all the way back to the lodge. He might as well stay the night.

Now that Joey had planned Chris's entire night for him, she decided she should probably tell him the plan. Once she finished her brownie. While snacking at the kitchen bar, she dug in her purse for her phone. One missed call from Kira. One missed text from Kira. Is the plan working? Are you over Ben yet? If not, stay under Chris. These things take time. One missed text from Chris. Feel free to make me miss lunch tomorrow, too.

Joey sent Chris a quick text in reply. If you haven't had dinner yet, you can come down to the cabin and skip that meal with me, too.

Who needs food? he quickly wrote back. Be there soon.

She grinned at the text. At least he wasn't angry at her for telling him no to the job offer. First time in her life she'd been offered a job while standing naked in a shower. If Chris's naked body couldn't convince her to take the job, nothing on earth would. Although she had been tempted. Of course she had. Coming back here for the wedding had been like coming home. She'd forgotten how much she missed this part of the world—the mountain, the rain that kept everything so lush and green even in fall and winter, the cottonwood trees turning as yellow as the sun this time of year, the scent of pine and fir, and her family, of course. Dillon in Portland. Mom and Dad only two and a half hours away in Tacoma. And the work would be fun, too. Marketing for a brand-new company just getting off the ground was a dream challenge. Not that it would be hard to convince people to come to Mount Hood and stay at Lost Lake. As soon as they saw the pictures of the area, they'd fall in love, madly in love. They would come here and never want to leave.

She knew how they felt.

And yet…she couldn't stay. Well, she could. But she *wouldn't* stay. She loved her job at Oahu Air, and she loved Honolulu, and she loved the work she did, and she did *not* want Ben to think for one single, solitary second that he was home free. If she quit her job, he won. After what he did to her and his wife, he didn't deserve to win. Kira was right, too. No way should she make a major life change so soon after a big breakup. If she took the job now, she'd be taking it for all the wrong reasons.

So that was that. She'd made up her mind. Might as well enjoy her time here while it lasted. She needed to store up as many good memories as she could to help her cope through the next few months of working with Ben. What would that mess be like? Would he ignore her? Would he try to win her back? Would he lie to her about what she saw? Would he beg her not to tell anyone? Would he find another woman at work to sleep with during his two weeks a month he spent in Hawaii? She could torture him a little, threaten to tell HR about them. Yes, she'd get fired but so would he. Almost worth it. Almost…

If only she could stop thinking about Ben. She didn't even miss him. She might have had it been a normal breakup where they decided their schedules were too incompatible or their goals in life too different. If the problem was that he wanted kids and she didn't it would be one thing, but this wasn't a normal breakup. The lying, the cheating… It ate at her. Staying busy kept her from dwelling on it too much, but as soon as she was alone again and had a split second to think, the anger came back to her again, hitting her like a slap in the face or a glass of ice water down the back of her shirt. A horrible feeling, sobering, simmering. She didn't want to feel this way. Not during this brief period she was back home with her family for such a happy occasion. Maybe if she called Ben and yelled at him she could get it out of her system. But she didn't want him to know he'd gotten to her this badly. Kira said to ignore him, let him go, pretend he meant nothing to her, and that would be the best of all revenges.

Kira was probably right about that, too. As much as Joey didn't want to let Ben off without at least verbally excoriating him, she knew that ultimately it didn't matter. The satisfaction of telling him off would be short-lived, and when it was all over and done with, she'd still have to get on with her life. Maybe if she skipped the dealing-with-Ben thing and headed straight into focusing on her own happiness, she'd find it a little faster.

Joey smiled as she heard the sound of a diesel engine pickup truck rambling down the gravel road toward the cabin. She never associated diesel engines with great sex before, but now that she'd started sleeping with Chris, they would be forever linked in her mind.

As she headed to the front door to unlock it, she

heard her phone vibrate on the walnut coffee table. It was a very loud wood. She picked up her phone and nearly answered on sheer instinct.

The call was from Ben.

She dropped the phone onto the sofa like it had burned her. The buzzing continued. At the front door she heard Chris's footsteps and then a soft knocking. Joey looked at the ringing phone. She turned and looked at the door. Her heart raced. Ben was calling her. For what? To scream at her? To apologize? To explain himself? To beg her not to tell HR on them? If he was calling her, he had something to say.

Joey picked up the phone off the couch and hit Decline.

Then she dropped it back on the coffee table and answered the door.

Ben could go fuck himself. He certainly wasn't going to get to fuck her anymore.

And speaking of fucking…

Joey answered the door and let Chris inside.

10

FOR THE EIGHTH morning in a row, Chris woke up in Joey's bed, although in his mind it was *his* bed since he'd made it with his own hands. A nice thought, Joey sleeping in *his* bed every single night. He did have his own bed at his place in Portland, but he much preferred staying with Joey in the cabin. It was closer to work, closer to the mountain and closer to every teenage dream he'd ever had about her. Back in high school he'd spent most of winter break here with them and most of summer break, too. This room had contained two sets of bunk beds and he and Dillon shared one and Joey took the other. Since she slept on the top bunk, Chris had, too, for no other reason that when the moon was bright or if he woke up early enough to catch the morning sun, he could see her sleeping not six feet away from him. He'd had a Nine Inch Nails T-shirt she'd latched on to for some reason and slept in it whenever she could steal it from the clean laundry basket. Maybe she'd just liked the color, although he pretended what she liked was the owner. When he saw her those summer mornings wearing his T-shirt, red-faced and rumpled and with a pillow over her eyes, he could pretend for a few seconds she was his girlfriend and this was their bedroom in their house and she loved him as much as he loved her, wanted him as much as he wanted her. Sadly, that particular erotic and romantic fantasy evaporated when Dillon let one rip in the middle of the night, which was when Chris regretted asking for the top bunk as both heat and horrible smells rose.

Upon reflection, watching Joey sleep as a teenager was a little creepy. He could admit that to himself. He made a lot of bad decisions at age seventeen and creeping on his best friend's sister was one of them. Of course now he was twenty-eight, and he was still watching her sleep. He couldn't blame that on being a horny lovesick teenager anymore. He had to blame it on being a horny lovesick grown man.

It was the eighth morning he'd spent the night in her bed, therefore it was the eighth morning in a row he'd had to stop himself from telling her the truth. He was falling in love with her already. Already and again. High school was ancient history so he tried to pretend his feelings were, too. But Mount Hood had sprung up five hundred thousand years ago, which made it ancient history, right? Yet there it was, its snowcap peeking above the treetops. Ancient history or not, it was there and undeniable. He could no more pretend he hadn't fallen back in love with Joey than he could pretend they weren't sleeping in a house on an active volcano. And something had to blow and soon because Joey was leaving in three days. Today was Thursday. The wedding was Saturday on Halloween. And Joey flew back to Hawaii on Sunday.

So he had all of today, Friday and Saturday to talk her into staying.

But first, he had to wake her up. He'd learned quickly the best way to wake Joey from a deep sleep was for him to leave the bed and start cooking breakfast. Poking and prodding and whispering would only elicit a groan from her before she flopped over onto her stomach and went immediately back to sleep.

If he cooked bacon, however…

No better alarm clock in the world.

Chris carefully slid Joey's arm off his stomach. She had an adorable habit of resting an arm or a leg across him while they slept. Well, it was adorable until he had to get out of bed to piss or go to work. Then it made the process slightly harrowing. He wanted to believe that the only sort of woman who would hold him in her sleep was a woman who was maybe possibly a little bit in love with him, too. Or maybe she was just one of those women who was always cold and therefore only used his naked body as a heat source. He'd assume the latter and hope for the former.

With good luck and good technique, Chris managed to slide out of bed without pulling Joey or the covers to the floor. She muttered something about it being too early before rolling over and going back to sleep again. He stood there a moment by the bed and took in the view. The view from the window was a sight to behold—lush, deep green fir trees, cottonwoods bright yellow in the morning sunlight, the white of the peak of Mount Hood and the moss growing on every tree trunk in sight. But none of that compared to the view inside the window, the view of Joey on her side, her beautiful naked back exposed and her hair lying wild on the pillow.

"I'm going to marry you by next Halloween," he said softly enough he knew she wouldn't hear even if she was awake.

Why did he promise he wouldn't try to make her stay?

Oh, yeah, because she wouldn't sleep with him if he didn't. She was right, though. She shouldn't be making huge decisions like quitting her job and moving so shortly after a breakup. He wasn't about to try to talk her into that. What he could do, however, was seduce her. Seduce her not for sex—that was already happening, a lot—but seduce her into staying. He wouldn't say a word about it. He'd let his seduction skills do the convincing and then Joey would decide to stay all on her own.

He'd start the seduction with bacon.

Chris pulled on his jeans and a T-shirt, and turned the heat up in the house. They both liked to sleep in a cool room under blankets. They didn't need the heat on to stay warm at night, anyway. They had each other for that.

Chris grinned to himself as he started cooking breakfast. He'd been grinning a lot lately, probably more in the past six days than in the last six months combined. All thanks to Joey and her sweet sexy self. Instead of spending her vacation hiking or biking or doing whatever people on vacations did—he wouldn't know as he hadn't taken one in four years—she came to work with him for part of the day and spent the rest of the day helping Dillon and Oscar with wedding stuff. She'd always been kind and selfless. She might tease Dillon and Oscar about getting married on her birthday but he knew she didn't care. She said she'd shared her birthday with Halloween and millions of trick-or-treaters every single year so it wasn't like she ever thought she owned the day. When she said she couldn't think of a better way to spend her birthday than watching her big brother get married to the love of his life, Chris knew she meant it.

"Is that bacon I smell?" Joey asked from the doorway. She had on his black-and-yellow checkered flannel shirt and slouchy mismatched wool socks and nothing else from what he could tell. One cheek bore a nice long pillow crease, and she'd pulled her hair back into a messy loose ponytail. Under her eyes were smudges left from eye makeup. He'd never seen a more beautiful sexy woman in all his born days.

"Bacon and eggs."

"You spoil me."

"It's what I was put on earth to do." He kissed her cheek as she leaned in to smell breakfast in the iron skillet.

"I'm starting to believe that."

She patted him on the ass as she went to the coffee pot for "fuel," as she called it. Fueling up, refueling, out of fuel. He was quickly learning all her quirks and habits. She couldn't go to sleep without flossing first no matter how tired she was. If she didn't she said she'd dream of her teeth falling out. She called all dogs, no matter how young or old, big or small, "puppies." When cleaning or doing laundry she sang Adele songs, just Adele. No one else. And she sang them badly. Very badly. She hated cilantro in her food, loved hot sauce on her eggs and would drive an hour just to get Stumptown Coffee Roasters coffee when they ran out of it. Rocket fuel, she called it. Her favorite.

"What are we doing today?" she asked between sips of rocket fuel.

"I'm done at Timber Ridge. Thought I'd take the day off."

"For me?" She batted her eyelashes at hm.

He carried the skillet with their bacon and eggs over to the table. She'd already set out the plates and forks. They made a good team in the kitchen.

"For you. If you want me. If you don't want me…" He took a step back, taking the bacon and eggs with him.

"I want you," she said. "I want you so much. And your bacon. All your bacon."

"You can have half my bacon. I get the other half."

"This is fair. I can accept this." She held up her plate and he scooped breakfast onto it. "You know, I'm only sleeping with you because you cook me breakfast every morning. I don't want you to think I actually like you or something."

"You're just using me for my bacon?"

"I am," she said, picking up a thick, crisp slice.

"That hurts." He sat down at the table across from her. "I'm hurt by that."

"Okay, maybe I'm not using you exclusively for your bacon."

"You can't just take something like that back," he said. "I'm wounded. To the core. I feel so…so used."

Joey leaned forward and rested her chin on her hand and stared at him across the table.

Then she held out her bacon to him.

"A gift?" he asked.

"Peace offering. And proof I'm not just using you for your bacon. Not exclusively."

He opened his mouth and she fed it to him.

"Good?" she asked.

"Tastes like love."

"Lust for sure," she said, wagging her eyebrows at him before taking another slice of bacon off her plate and stirring hot sauce into her eggs.

Chris picked up his fork and focused on his eating and tried to ignore that Joey had brushed aside his use of the L-word with a quick joke. Not that he blamed her. She'd gotten out of a two-year-long relationship last week. In her shoes he wouldn't even be dating someone else, much less considering a future with them. But he wasn't in her shoes. He was in his shoes. And the man in his shoes was quickly falling in love with the woman in Joey's shoes. Well, socks. Wait, were those his socks, too?

"So…there's this thing in the sky today," Chris said. "Have you seen it?"

"What is it?"

"It's big and it's yellow and it's very bright."

"Big Bird?"

"Not quite."

"A very large honeydew melon?"

"Hotter. I think it might be the sun."

"No way."

"Way."

"Are you sure?" Joey asked. "Doesn't sound like anything you'd see in Lost Lake in October."

"I double-checked. It's there. Still. And it doesn't seem to be going away for the next couple of hours. I think we should do something with it. In it, I mean."

"Like worship it? Sacrifice someone or something to it?"

"Or we could walk to the lake and around the lake. I hear this is a thing people do when the sun is out."

"Sounds good," she said. "Good excuse to wear my cute new hiking boots. Not a lot of excuses to wear boots on a beach."

"Visit more often and you can boot around all you want."

"Maybe I will. For the boots," she said, and winked at him. "I'll go get ready."

Joey left to get dressed while Chris hunted down his shoes and jacket. Last night Joey had been all over him the second he'd walked through the front door. They'd had sex on the sofa first with the fireplace roaring a few feet away. They'd had sex in the bed an hour later. Well, on the bed if not in the bed. He'd put Joey's hands on the headboard and fucked her from behind. One of his favorite positions as he could have total access to every inch of the front of her body while inside her. The question was…at what point during last night's fuck fest had he taken his work boots off?

Chris found his boots under the sofa. So apparently he'd taken them off after the first fucking and before the second fucking. When he and Joey both had their clothes on—such a pity—they walked out the back door and headed down the muddy path through the trees.

"You remember how to get to the lake?" she asked as he took her hand.

"I know exactly where we're going."

"Then why did you take the right fork when the left fork leads to the lake?"

"Because we're not going to the lake just yet. I want to show you something."

Joey raised her eyebrow.

"Not that," he said. "You've already seen it."

"I know, but I never get tired of the view."

Chris laughed as he dragged her by the hand down the path. Sunlight trickled through the high canopy of towering Douglas firs and red cedar trees. Ferns and bear grass lined the edge of the trail like a soft green fence. The last week of rain had left the trails muddy and the air scented with pine and cedar and everything clean and alive. Impossible to walk this path with this woman and not give in to the voice of hope inside him that said even if Joey wouldn't stay in Oregon for him, maybe she would stay for this day, this land, this mountain, this lake.

"This cabin," Chris said when they reached the end of the path. "Like it?"

"Wow." Joey let go of his hand and stepped into the clearing. "Oh, my God…"

"Good reaction."

"It's Thoreau's cabin."

"Not quite, but close. I found pictures of it when I restored it and went off those."

Joey turned to face him, her dark eyes wide, her mouth slightly open. Took all his strength not to kiss the life out of her.

"You did this?"

"It was on its last legs," Chris said. "It was either tear it down completely or rebuild it from the studs up. Seemed like a good contender for a stone facade."

"You did this?" she asked again. "All you?"

"Not all me. I hired a few subcontractors. But the redesign was all me."

"It's incredible. I used to dream about living in a cottage like this."

"I know. You had pictures of those Carmel-by-the-Sea fairy-tale cottages on your Wonder Wall."

"You remember my Wonder Wall?"

"I remember hating Oasis and rolling my eyes that you called your collage in your room your 'Wonder Wall.'"

"I was fourteen. I didn't even know who Oasis was. I just liked the song. And what were you doing peeking at my dream collage, anyway?"

"I wanted to see if I was on it."

"Were you?"

"No. Harry Potter was."

"I'd still spread for Daniel Radcliffe."

"Do you want to see inside this cabin or do you want to make me puke?" he asked.

"I want to see inside."

He took her by the hand again and led her up the cobblestone path to the front door. He'd found some photos online of stone cabins and cottages and had painted the windowsills bright red with a red front door.

"We went to Carmel when I was a kid," she said. "Best vacation. I loved all those little houses."

"You sent me a postcard."

"I did?"

"You don't remember?"

"I sent tons of postcards," she said.

"I feel so special."

She looked at him and smiled. "You are special."

"Write it on a postcard. Maybe then I'll believe that."

Joey wrapped her arms around his neck and kissed him long and hard on the mouth. Tongue was involved. Very involved.

"Now do you feel special?" she asked.

"The special-est. Now stop kissing me so I can find the keys."

She stepped back and he dug around in his pockets, producing a key ring of many, many keys.

"How many houses do you have?"

"I have keys to all the Lost Lake properties," he said, flipping to the key with the red tag. "I'm Dillon's personal handyman."

"Thought that was Oscar."

"I'm going to tell them both you said that."

He stuck the key in the lock, opened the door, and like the gentleman he usually wasn't, he let Joey in first. He flipped on the light switch and shut the door behind them.

"It's not finished," he said. "We had to focus on the exterior and the roof before the weather turned."

Joey stood in the center of house and spun in one complete circle.

"It's so beautiful I can't even believe it's real. I thought you worked a miracle with Mom and Dad's old cabin. This is…"

"This is what it looked like." Chris pulled out his phone and scrolled until he found his pictures.

"Holy…"

"More like hole-y. Mouse holes everywhere. Holes in the floor. Holes in the roof. It's a slate roof now."

"I have no idea what that is but it looks awesome. The whole place looks like my dream come true."

Chris only nodded, proud of his handiwork. The

work spoke for itself. He'd put in cedar paneling, diamond rectangle windows by either side of the fireplace, and replaced the old crumbling stone fireplace with red brick to match the windowsills and door. All lighting came from wall sconces he'd picked up at thrift stores and vintage shops and he'd bought the rug on the floor from a local weaver who called herself a "fiber artist," whatever that was. She made damn good rugs.

"I'm glad you like it," Chris said. It was all he could think to say. Joey made him feel all kinds of something—proud and speechless and embarrassed and in love all at once. The less he said, the better. Otherwise, he might let it slip that he was in love with her already.

"I love it. I just… I absolutely love it."

"I'm glad. I wanted you to see it. Maybe you can stay in this cabin next time you're in town."

"That's the second time in thirty minutes you mentioned me coming back to town."

"Just saying…you should visit more often."

"Or move back?"

"I didn't say that."

"Chris, I can't stay. We talked about this."

"I didn't ask you to stay. I'm just showing you how nice it is here so maybe you'll visit more often. That's all."

"I'll visit more often or I'll stay?"

"No comment. But…do you want to see the other eight houses we own? The other eight cabins I turned into cabins like this?" He grinned at her wickedly.

"That's so not fair."

"When you visit again you can stay in any of our cabins that aren't booked."

"If the other cabins are half as beautiful as this one,

you won't have any trouble at all keeping them booked," Joey said.

"That's probably true. They are pretty damn good cabins."

"I'm sure they are."

"Although they do need a good decorator."

"Now you're just being evil."

Chris laughed. "I knew that would get you. I remember you were always making me and Dillon move furniture for you."

"Never give a fourteen-year-old girl a book on feng shui."

"You see anything missing from this cabin?"

"Furniture. Dishes. A manual typewriter."

"A manual typewriter?"

"Yes." She pointed at an empty wall. "This cabin… it looks like Thoreau's on Walden Pond. I'd market this cabin as an artist's retreat. You couldn't comfortably sleep more than two people in here, anyway, right?"

"Two hundred square feet. Pretty tight fit."

"But one artist or one writer…perfect. I'd market direct to artist colonies and MFA programs. People who paint *en plein air* and people who dreamed of writing a book and never got around to starting one. You put a big wooden desk over here. Manual typewriter here. Some inspirational artwork on the walls. A bookcase here with dictionaries and stuff like that."

"People can get dictionaries online."

"No." She shook her head. "Not online. This cabin shouldn't have internet access. None."

"None?"

"None. No distractions. No internet. No Wi-Fi. No television. Only one phone, the kind with cords and dial tones. And maybe a radio but an old radio. Art deco style. Can you get any cell service out here?"

Chris pulled out his phone again and checked the bars.

"None."

"See? Perfect writer retreat. I can see it now."

"So…fewer amenities? This is your advice?"

"People go on vacation to get away from it all. Now because of the internet and cell phones, all that 'all' they're trying to get away from comes with them. Go after the people who really want to get away. The people who just want nothing more than to be on a mountain in the woods by a lake, surrounded by all the beauty—"

"You're talking about me, right? I know. You don't have to say it."

"Surrounded by natural beauty—which you are… yes, it's helped. It's helped more than I can say. You can't run away from your problems but you can leave them for a while. I think that's what this place should be. This little Lost Lake Village cabin here? Make it a real sanctuary. Going a few days without the internet and CNN never killed anyone, but it probably could save someone's sanity. Or marriage. Or inspire someone to finally write that first page of their novel."

"Even my dad says he wants to write a book someday about his tour in the army. And sometimes I leave my phone in the truck overnight just to be left alone. I can see it working."

"Everybody thinks they want to write a book. Or paint. Or write nature poetry. Or just get away from the world for a while. Away from Twitter and Facebook and all the noise. A tiny cabin in the woods with no internet access, no TV… People would pay a premium for that. There are already hotels popping up that cater to those people. Why not a cabin at Lost Lake? Get lost to find yourself."

"Get lost to find yourself. There's our slogan. That's fucking genius, Jo."

"Thank you." She playfully brushed her hair off her forehead. "This is why they pay me those big marketing bucks."

"And you wonder why Dillon wants to hire you."

"I know why he wants to hire me—because he's a genius. But I've already got a job. I can help while I'm here, though. So…today and tomorrow?"

"Great. I can give you the company credit card to go buy all the stuff we need. The desk, the typewriter, dictionaries, anything you think would work." Maybe if Joey got to play at doing the job for one day she'd realize it was what she should be doing. Maybe. Hopefully. Worth a shot, right?

"You'd let me buy whatever I want for this cabin?"

"I remember your Wonder Wall. You have a good eye," Chris said. And a good everything else.

"I know something good when I see it," she said, walking over to him.

"Do you?"

"Obviously I do." She put her hands on his shoulders and kissed the side of his neck. Chris closed his eyes and inhaled deeply.

Chris ran his hands down her back. She felt warm through her sweater, warm and right. She belonged here. Not here in Oregon. Not here in Lost Lake. Not here in this cabin. But here, in his hands. Her body. His hands. That's where Joey belonged.

"I should withhold sex until you agree to come back and visit me. Like, ASAP."

"That would probably work right about now," she said. "I might agree to anything if you told me you wouldn't sleep with me again until I agreed to it."

"I wish I were that tough."

"You're not?"

"Nope…" He pulled her to him and turned her in one swift motion. "I'm weak. So weak."

He took her by the wrists and lifted her arms, pressing her wrists into the wall. Joey playfully struggled against him and gave up quickly.

"If this is your version of weak…"

"What about it?" he asked.

"Then I love it when you're weak."

Chris kissed her hard enough to make her whimper. He wasn't the sort of man who believed in luck. Hard work? Yes. Good timing? Sure. But pure dumb luck? Not until now. Once upon a time he picked a desk at random in a classroom on the first day of school and the desk next to him was claimed by a guy named Dillon wearing a Pearl Jam shirt and it felt like destiny. And now, years later, here he was, kissing the most beautiful woman the world, about to have sex with the most beautiful woman in the world, madly in love with the most beautiful woman in the world. And she'd leave him in three days. So not only did Chris believe in luck, he believed in bad luck.

But for now all he'd think about was the good luck that brought Joey and him here—what they had in the moment, not what they'd lose in three days. And maybe, just maybe, if he made this good enough for her, she would stay. Wishful thinking? Yeah, but what other choice did he have?

Chris slid his hands under her sweater and unclasped her bra in the back. He knew his hands were cold—the cabin itself was chilly—and it gave him a perverse sort of pleasure to put his cold fingers onto her bare breasts. She gasped, shivered and laughed.

"Asshole…" she said.

"Just warming up my hands. Do you mind?" He took her breasts in his hands and lightly kneaded them. He brushed his thumbs over her nipples and they hardened. This was a woman who loved being touched and he was a man who loved touching her. Obviously they belonged together.

He lifted her shirt and bent his head to lick her right nipple. Her hands twined in his hair and she held him against her breast as he sucked her and sucked her. Both of his hands held and squeezed both of her breasts. He couldn't get enough of them, enough of her. While he distracted her by grazing her nipple with this teeth, he unbuttoned her jeans and pushed down the zipper.

"Don't you dare put your cold fingers on my—"

That was as far as she got before he slipped his hand into her panties and touched her clitoris.

The sound she made could be replicated only by a bird or a dog whistle. He had no idea humans could make sounds in a register that high. Impressive. Amazing the windows didn't shatter.

"You're a monster." She sighed.

"I know."

"The worst."

"The absolute worst," he agreed. He rubbed her the way he knew she liked, softly in a circle. She moved

with his hand and he felt her clitoris swelling. Gently
he eased a finger back and inside her, touching her wetness. He loved that wetness, loved that he could do that
to her, for her. When she was wet like this, he could
slide his fingers deep into her. And she wasn't just wet,
she was hot inside. He caressed the front wall of her vagina and felt her inner muscles clenching at his fingers.
He pulled his finger out of her and rubbed the wetness
onto her clitoris. Joey cried out, close to coming. She
clung to his shoulders, her nails digging in hard enough
he could feel them through the thick flannel fabric of
his shirt. His erection was already trying to get his attention. He ignored it for now.

"Pure...evil..." She panted the words as he stroked
her with one hand while the other eased her jeans down
her hips, down her thighs. Finally, he just gave up and
pushed them to the floor. Joey kicked off her shoes and
sent her pants flying halfway across the cabin.

"I like your enthusiasm," he said.

"Why aren't you inside me yet?"

"Are you that horny?"

"I'm cold. I need your body heat."

"I'm touched. Truly."

Joey stuck her hands in his pants, her ice cold hands.

"Now you're touched," she said, rubbing his cock.
"Truly."

"You're in so much trouble for that."

"Good. Getting in trouble warms me up."

Chris pulled his wallet from his pocket and dug out
the condom he'd thankfully stored in there earlier this
week. Joey seemed intent on torturing him so she kissed
and sucked lightly on his earlobe while he rolled on
the condom. When it was on he grabbed her by the

upper arms and pushed her against the wall again. She squealed.

"What?" he demanded.

"Cold wall. Cold butt."

"Such a big baby," he said. "Here. This better?" He cupped her ass in his now-warm hands and she sighed with pleasure.

"So much better. Now what?"

"Put your arms around my neck, tight."

She did as instructed. Being in charge during sex got him off like nothing else. And that Joey liked it? Even loved it? How could he let her get on that plane to Hawaii on Sunday? Unless it was to go back and pack? More wishful thinking…

He lifted her left leg up and stroked her pussy with the tip of his cock. He kissed her mouth, her neck, her throat, all while rubbing his cock against her. When she started to open up to him he pushed the tip inside. She moved her hips into his, rocking him deeper inside her. Without a word of warning, he lifted her and brought her all the way down onto him. Joey groaned, a gorgeous sound, and wrapped her entire body around him. Both legs, both arms, her chin on his shoulder, her mouth at his ear. With his hands firmly on her ass, he held her to him, rocking his hips into her as he fucked her against the wall. In this position he knew he wouldn't last very long. Luckily it didn't seem like Joey would need him to. The way she moved right now, her lower body working against his hard and hungry, was a clear sign she was close to coming already. He pushed into her with strong but controlled thrusts.

"God, Chris. It feels so good," Joey said into his ear.

"You want it?"

"I want it. All the time."

"You can have it all the time. Whenever you want. Just ask for it and it's yours."

"Now?"

"Now."

"Tomorrow?"

"Every day of your life," he said, thrusting deep again. She clenched around his cock and he knew she was almost there. With a series of rapid thrusts he pushed her the rest of the way. With a whimper in his ear and her fingernails in his neck, she came all around him. He kept thrusting until he came with a loud groan. The pleasure of it wrecked him, sent him reeling. He set Joey carefully down on her feet but didn't let her go. He rested his forehead on her shoulder, his hands on her waist.

"Why do you insist on making me feel so good?" she asked, running her hands up his arms. She laughed a little, the question obviously rhetorical. Chris decided to answer it, anyway.

"Because I'm in love with you."

11

IF CHRIS HAD told her he was dying, Joey would have been less shocked.

"What?" She pushed away from him, found her pants and pulled them on as quickly as she could. Chris stood by the wall, facing it as he pulled himself together.

"You heard me," was all he said. She watched as he straightened his clothes, ran his hands through his hair that she'd mussed with her own hands during the sex.

"You're in love with me?"

"Is it that big of a surprise?" He turned around and faced her, calm as ever. So infuriatingly calm. He crossed his arms over his chest, leaned against the wall, waited.

"Well…yeah. I'm leaving on Sunday and you tell me this now?"

"When should I have told you?"

"Not now. Not…ever?"

"You asked."

"I was joking."

"I wasn't."

"What am I supposed to do with this?" she asked, taking a step back.

He shrugged his shoulders. "Anything. Nothing."

"Anything or nothing. Good choices there."

"It's your choice. I said it. What you want to do with it is up to you."

Joey's hands shook and her heart raced. Panic. What she felt was pure panic. How could he be so fucking calm while she stood here in an absolute panic?

"You promised me, Chris. You promised me you wouldn't do this. No, you didn't promise me. You swore."

"I swore on a fucking CD, not the Bible."

"I don't care if you swore on a bowl of oatmeal or a pack of gum or your own grave, you swore to me you wouldn't make it weird. You swore you wouldn't ask me to stay."

"I didn't ask you to stay. I told you I loved you."

"You made it real fucking weird, though."

"You asked me and I answered. I'm in love with you. So what? If you're not in love with me, I don't know what the problem is."

"This is so fucking unfair, Chris."

Chris laughed, and for the first time since laying eyes on him a week ago, Joey regretted coming home.

"Fair? What does fairness have to do with it?"

"You're trying to keep me from going back home."

"I'm not trying to make you do anything. I don't want you to leave, but I'm not making you stay," he said.

"I never figured you for the manipulative type, Chris. I have to say this is pretty fucking disappointing."

"Well…welcome to my world. I tell you I love you.

You get mad and accuse me of manipulating you. *Disappointing* is a damn good word for it."

"I have a home and a job in another state."

"You can have a home and a job in this state if you wanted it."

"*You* can have a home and a job in another state," she said. "Why don't *you* quit your job and move to Hawaii if you think it's so easy."

"Is that an invitation?"

"No. It is not. You know you wouldn't do it. You know you wouldn't uproot your entire world to be with me." She shoved her feet back into her shoes, angry, flustered, scared.

"I do? You sure about that?"

"I'm sure about that."

"Try me."

"I'm not trying anything," she said. "I'm not even having this conversation with you."

"Why not? What are you afraid of?"

She raised her hand and pointed at him. "Nothing. I'm not afraid of anything."

"Are you afraid of falling in love with me? If you are, you don't have to be. I'm not Ben. You won't be my backup plan. You won't be a dirty secret. I'm not a liar like he is."

"You are a liar. You swore you wouldn't do this to me and here you are—doing it."

"Good pain," he said. "Remember? We agreed on that. We both knew this would end up hurting us and we decided to do it, anyway. I knew you were using me as your rebound guy. You knew I was in love with you in high school. We've been together day and night for almost two weeks. You can't be surprised by this, can you? Are you?"

"You're hurting me, Chris."

"I'm loving you. Right now. This second. I love you. And I'm sorry it hurts you but guess what? It hurts me, too."

"You don't look hurt." No, he didn't look hurt at all. He looked fine. Just fucking fine. Meanwhile she wanted to scream or cry or kiss him or slap him and she hated that he could be calm in a moment like this when she couldn't.

"What does hurt look like?"

"Like this." She turned her back on him and walked out of the cabin, slamming the beautiful red door behind her.

She should have known.

She should have known this would happen.

In fact, she *had* known it would happen. That's why she told Chris a week ago at the lodge they were playing with fire. That's why she'd made him swear he wouldn't make it harder for her. How stupid was he to think telling her he loved her wouldn't make it harder?

It wasn't supposed to be like this. It was supposed to be great sex and friendship and then she'd leave and they'd sigh a little wistfully and they'd both get on with their lives. Chris was one of those guys who always seemed okay. Anything that happened to him was just water off a duck's back. Quiet, strong, hardworking, resilient. Fine. Chris was fine. He was always fine. He'd fought off high school bullies without breaking a sweat. When mocked at school for being best friends with the supposedly only gay kid in school, he'd shrugged it off without a word. She trusted Chris, which is why it had been so easy to let herself believe she could sleep with him for a couple weeks and walk away with no permanent damage to either of them. A few tears, a few regrets, sure. But Chris was in love with her and he told her that knowing it would make her the bad guy when she walked away.

Fine, then. She'd be the bad guy.

She trudged down the path back toward the cabin. The muddy path wanted to slow her down but she wouldn't let it.

Men. Fucking men. They were allowed to be married to their jobs, married to their careers, but God forbid a woman picked her job over the man in her life. God forbid she says, "Nope, my job's more important than you are." Oh, no. That's not what women were allowed to do. A guy tells her he loves her and she's supposed to drop everything, run into his arms and say, "Thank you for making my life worth living with your love. I was just over here doing nothing but running the marketing department of a successful airline while living in a tropical paradise, but now that I know you love me, I can stop wasting my time with that whole stupid life and career thing. By the way, how many babies can I have for you and how do you want your eggs cooked every morning, Master?"

And how dare Chris accuse her of being scared. Her? Scared? She was the one who went to college across a fucking ocean. He lived with his parents after high school graduation. She wasn't afraid of anything except maybe killing Chris the next time she saw him, which would hopefully be never. Chris was supposed to be her date for Dillon's wedding.

Well, forget that. She'd rather skip the wedding than see him again.

Afraid?

Her?

He didn't know the meaning of the word if he thought that. Just because he'd said he loved her? Why would she be afraid of him loving her? Oh, maybe because the man she'd been in love with for the past two years had lied to her the entire time they were together, had betrayed her so deeply she wasn't sure she'd ever find the bottom of the wound he'd left in her pride and her heart. Maybe because Chris was everything she'd ever wanted and never realized it until she came back here and if she were going to have what she'd wanted she'd have to give up everything she had.

Joey stopped and leaned against a tree. She'd been walking so fast and so hard she was out of breath. One second, that's all she needed. Maybe a minute. She was fine. Only needed to breathe. Joey breathed and breathed.

And then she cried. No. Not this. She didn't want to start crying again. If she started crying again she might not stop. But she couldn't stop. It all came out. Big heavy sobs. Deep belly weeping. Gasping for air. Holding her stomach. Pain in her ribs. A stitch in her side. Fat tears by turns hot and cold on her face. A terrible bitter taste in her mouth.

Fucking men… Was she not even a human being to them? Was she just a toy for Ben to play with while in Hawaii? Was she still fourteen to Chris? Where did they get off kicking her heart around like a soccer ball? She didn't do that to them. She didn't make Ben choose between LA and Hawaii. She didn't rat him out to his wife. She didn't tell Chris if he really loved her he'd move to Hawaii to be with her. And how dare he even pretend he would if she asked him to? He didn't get to do that. Chris didn't get to play Mr. Wonderful while she was forced into the role of The One Who Got Away just because he decided to dump a declaration of love on her ten days after a breakup and three days before she left town. It wasn't fair. It wasn't right. And it wasn't like Chris.

Now, Ben would do something like that. And he had, too. He'd forced her into being The Other Woman without her knowledge or permission. She'd be the butt of awful office gossip at work if and when it got out that a) she and Ben had dated, and b) he was married. She hadn't chosen that, either.

Joey pushed away from the tree and headed down the path again. She wasn't going to spend the entire day weeping in the forest like some kind of Disney princess waiting on woodland creatures to gather around her. With her luck she'd end up being "comforted" by a black bear or a mountain lion.

As she walked up the path she made a decision. No more playing house with Chris. They were fools to think they could sleep together, hang out together, work together, play together and then just say "Later!" at the airport and go their separate ways without it hurting the both of them. Joey couldn't even rip off a Band-Aid without losing a little skin. To say goodbye to Chris would take off more than one layer of her heart and it was an open wound already.

So…it was over. Completely over. She could spend today and tomorrow miserable, then she'd put on a happy face for the wedding, leave on Sunday and that was that. The next few months would be hellish, of course, but she'd known that before leaving LA. When she got to work Monday morning, there was a very good chance Ben would be there, in her office, waiting to hash it out with her. And she would simply hand him a box of the stuff he'd left at her apartment and say goodbye. If he tried anything, anything at all, she would call HR and tell them everything. This would, of course, get her and Ben fired but that wouldn't be the end of the world. Her boyfriend of two years was married. She'd discovered this by coming face-to-face with his wife. She'd met the greatest guy in the world while on the rebound and she had to leave him on Sunday. Why shouldn't she also get fired? When it rains it pours and nobody knew that better than somebody born and raised in the Pacific Northwest.

But staying here was out of the question.

Staying meant Ben won. And the sort of man who would cheat on his wife and lie to his girlfriend didn't get to win. There had to be consequences even if they were just seeing her at work every day and knowing she had the power to get him fired anytime she wanted. That's what a man like Ben deserved. A cheater. A liar. A coward. And if he were here she'd tell him that to his face.

Joey left the main path and strode up the cobblestone walkway to the cabin. She went in the back door and kicked off her muddy shoes. They hit the wall with a thud. Another thud followed, but it hadn't come from her shoes.

Someone knocked on the door, paused and knocked again.

Joey sighed. Chris must know a shortcut back to

the cabin. She didn't want to talk to him yet, but she couldn't keep him out of the cabin. He'd left some stuff in the bathroom. And now that she'd blown off a little steam she could probably talk to him without yelling or crying. Or if not talk to him at least she should give him his toothbrush back.

She took a deep breath, wiped the tears off her face and opened the door.

Joey's heart dropped down her body, into the floor and landed at the center of the earth.

"Hey, Jo."

She couldn't believe her eyes. She didn't want to believe them. But she had to believe them because there he was, right there, right on the porch of the cabin.

Joey lifted her chin and met Ben's eyes.

"What the hell are you doing here?"

12

"Nice way to say hi," Ben said.

"That's exactly what you said to me when I came to visit you. Word for word."

"Yeah, I'm sorry about that. Can I come in?"

"No, you can't come in. How the hell did you even find me, anyway?" She could not believe he was here. Ben. Here. In the forest. On the mountain. In Oregon. He looked so out of place she would laugh if she didn't want to cry and scream so much. He had on a suit. A business suit and a long, khaki-colored Burberry coat with a jaunty red scarf around his neck. Did he buy all that stuff just for this one trip to the Pacific Northwest? Probably, knowing him.

"You told me you were staying at your parents' old cabin. It's not that hard to look up addresses and deeds online."

"Stalker."

"Jesus, Jo, we practically lived together two years. I called five times a day. You never answered any calls, any texts. I have no idea how you are, what you're doing. You could have at least texted me back."

"You don't get to tell me what I should do. Ever. I don't even know why you're here. I didn't invite you."

"Can we not talk for five minutes?"

Joey pulled her phone out of her back pocket, opened the alarm app and started the stopwatch.

"Five minutes," she said, holding up her phone to show him the quickly passing numbers. "Go."

"You're in a bad mood."

"That's a great way to use up four seconds of your time."

"Shit, fine. Okay." He ran a hand through his perfectly coiffed black hair and looked around the porch as if seeking help or inspiration. "I don't know where to start."

"You can start by telling me why you didn't tell me you were married," she said. "You are married, right? That was your wife? She had a wedding ring on and she called you her husband. But I admit she could have been delusional and/or hallucinating. Stranger things have happened."

"She is my wife, yes. I'm married, yes. I didn't tell you because…"

"I'm waiting."

"Look, Shannon and I have an open marriage. We have for a long time."

"Good for you both. But I don't."

"You aren't married."

"I don't have an open anything," she said. "I don't do open relationships."

"I figured. That's why I didn't tell you. You're not the sort of woman who'd ever date a married man even in an open marriage. That's why I didn't tell you."

"Oh, so is this a compliment or an insult? I can't tell.

Either I have too much integrity to date a married man or I'm too close-minded and vanilla to date someone in an open marriage? Which one is it?"

"It's neither. It's… I don't know. I just didn't want to tell you. I'm married in LA. I'm not married in Hawaii. That's my life."

She narrowed her eyes at him.

"You know that's not how marriage works, right? I mean, even if it does in your world, legally you are still married in Hawaii."

"That's just the rule we came up with. Shannon has a boyfriend."

"Good for Shannon. More power to her. Does her boyfriend know about you?"

"Yeah, but—"

"So your wife has more integrity than you do. Congrats on marrying up. And you're down to two minutes so speed it up."

Ben turned his back to her and for a second she thought he'd leave right then and there.

"I'm sorry," he said.

"What?" She couldn't believe she heard that right. Ben turned around and faced her again.

"I'm sorry. I was an idiot."

"Yes, you were."

"I was…am crazy about you. Have been since I saw you. Something told me that if you knew about me and Shan, even knowing we had an open marriage, you wouldn't want to get involved with me. So I didn't tell you."

"For two years."

"How was I supposed to bring that up, Jo? Take you

out to dinner and over dessert say, 'By the way, I'm married but it's okay'?"

"You could have tried that. I would have thrown my wine in your face, probably still in the glass. But it would have been better than showing up on your doorstep and meeting the missus. She didn't look happy to see me. You sure she knew about the open marriage?"

"She did. But we have a rule about that sort of thing."

"What sort of thing?"

"Not having our significant others over to our house."

"Oh, I'm sorry. Did I invade your marital sanctuary? I would never have done that had I known your rule. Or that you were married. Or that you were a walking, talking human piece of shit."

"Joey."

"Fuck you."

"You're out of line."

"You don't get to talk to me anymore. Go away."

"This isn't like you. This isn't the Joey I know."

"You aren't the Ben I know. The Ben I know isn't married. You are a sleazy married guy who lies to everyone so he can have all the sex he wants with all the women he wants. No one at work knew you were married. Don't pretend you kept it a secret just from me. Don't act like I'm the first woman you slept with without telling her you were married."

"I shouldn't have come here."

"No, you shouldn't have. No idea why you did."

"I came here to tell you I love you, that I'm sorry and that if you want me I'll get a divorce."

"You'll get a divorce."

"Yes. For you."

"You'll get a divorce. For me."

"And we could get married. Maybe. Eventually. When you stop hating me."

Ben stepped forward. She stepped back.

"I will never stop hating you."

"Jo, stop. I'm not a monster. I lied. I admit it. It was bad. Really, really bad, but I'm not the enemy."

"You're bringing up marriage to me while you're still married."

"Shannon and I haven't been great together in a few years. It was one reason we agreed to the open marriage thing. Nothing is getting better, though."

"My heart breaks for you."

"You're furious. I get it. I'll go and you can think about it. When you're calm, we can talk again."

"I am furious. And yes, you should go."

Ben stepped down off the porch.

"You know…" Ben pointed his finger at her and smiled. "You wouldn't be this angry with me if you didn't have such strong feelings. Hate's just the flip side of love. Think about that."

Joey returned the smile.

"I've been fucking someone else all week. Think about that," she said, pointing back at him.

Ben stumbled on the bottom step.

"You what?"

"Since the day I got here. I'm seeing someone."

"I don't believe this." He turned his back on her but only for a second. "You're not kidding, are you?"

"I did dump you so why not, right?"

"You didn't dump me, Jo. You ran off. You got into a cab and drove off and haven't said one word to me about breaking up with me."

"I think you being married means it goes without

saying. Of course I broke up with you. We're over. Forever."

"You should have told me," Ben said.

"You don't get to tell me what I should and shouldn't do. You have no right to judge me at all."

"I never once cheated on my wife. Ask her. It's not cheating. But what you did—"

"I didn't cheat on you, darling," she said with a saccharine smile. "Didn't you know? You and I were in an open relationship. I just didn't tell you."

"Oh, very funny. Hilarious."

"Why are you still here? Your five minutes are up."

"I'm going. Hope you and your rebound boy are very happy together."

"We are."

Those two words came from Chris, not Joey. Chris stepped around the house to the porch and looked at her.

"Sorry, Joey," he said. "I wasn't eavesdropping. I just need my keys from in the cabin."

"Right. Of course," she said. "Door's unlocked."

Chris strode right past Ben without saying a word to him, without making eye contact, without acknowledging his existence. Ben didn't speak, either, and she didn't doubt why. Chris wasn't huge but he didn't look like the sort of man a guy in a thousand-dollar suit would want to antagonize especially when those steel-toed work boots of his made a heavy echoing sound on the steps of the porch. All that was missing was a pair of spurs to add a Wild West jingle.

Chris went into the cabin leaving her and Ben alone again.

"Him," Ben said.

"Him," Joey said. "He's a contractor. Old friends of ours from high school. Used to break noses for Dillon."

"As a hobby?"

"Because assholes and bullies wanted to kill my brother in high school and Chris protected him."

"You're threatening me with your new boyfriend."

"No. I'm just telling you who he is."

"Nice beard. The flannel's a good touch. Very authentic. What do they call those guys—lumbersexuals?"

"Men, Ben. They're called 'men.'"

Ben stared at her, angry. She knew angry and he was angry.

"What about work?" he asked.

"What about it?"

"We work together."

"Not much."

"You going to tattle on me?"

"It crossed my mind."

"You know if they can me they can you, too. Takes two to tango."

"I've already been offered another job."

"You're not going to take it, are you?"

"Haven't decided yet."

"You're going to let this hang over my head, aren't you? Just to punish me? Very mature."

"Let me ask you a question and you give me an honest answer," Joey said. "Do you really think you deserve better?"

He didn't answer at first. She gave him credit for that.

"No," he finally said.

She gave him credit for that, too.

"You should go," she said.

"Yeah, I can see that. Going."

"Anything of yours that's not out of my apartment by the time I get back Sunday night will go to Goodwill or the dump. Leave your key on the kitchen table."

He turned to walk away and did walk away. He made it halfway down the path to his car before turning back around again.

"I did love you, you know. I do love you," Ben said.

"Then you should have been honest with me."

"Is your new boy honest with you?"

"Too honest," she said.

"Goddamn, you're hard to please, aren't you?"

"I have high standards. Getting higher all the time."

"Well, good luck finding your Mr. Right. Tell your new boyfriend good luck. He'll need it."

With that parting shot, Ben walked away and didn't turn back. He got into his rental car and drove away. For a minute or two she heard the sound of his wheels on the gravel getting fainter and fainter. Not that long ago she would have cried when Ben told her, *Goodbye, see you in a couple weeks, love you, be good, baby, I'll be back soon…*

They'd had so many farewells and reunions dating him had been like riding a roller coaster. Every goodbye a stomach-churning dip. Every reunion a heart-pounding high. They'd never had a real stable and solid relationship, did they? She knew that now. Just one honeymoon after the other. She knew she was over him not because the anger was all gone—it wasn't—but because she didn't cry as he left, and she knew she'd never cry for him again. He wasn't worth her tears. He wasn't worth her time. Maybe he wasn't even worth punishing anymore.

"Is he gone?" Chris asked from the doorway.

"Gone."

"You okay?"

"I'm okay."

"Good." He shut the door behind him. "I'll go, too. I'll…"

Joey tensed, scared of what he would say, scared of what she should say but didn't have the words yet.

"Wedding's on Saturday. Do you still want to go with me?"

"I can't be Sam without Farmer Ted, can I?" she asked.

Chris smiled but it wasn't a happy smile, not at all.

"I'll see you at the wedding, then? Or should I pick you up?"

She wanted him to pick her up. She wanted everything to go back to normal between them for her last couple of days in Oregon before heading back to Hawaii. Why did it have to change? It had been so good. They'd had dinner with her parents two nights ago— her and Chris and Dillon and Oscar and Mom and Dad and…it had been perfect. Like old times but better because no one was scared for Dillon anymore. Mom and Dad had even behaved themselves and not brought up her breakup with Ben at dinner. Joey had seen knowing smiles between her and Dad as if they were saying, "Hmm…looks like somebody is getting a little help getting over her boyfriend…" The whole time Chris's knee pressed against hers and his hand squeezed her hand between courses. She'd felt like she and Chris were a real couple that night, as much of a couple as Dillon and Oscar, who were getting married in a few days, and her parents, who'd been married thirty years. Chris fit right into the family. Her mom had even kissed both his cheeks and her dad had hugged him. Dad did not hug other men unless they were his own father or his son. Or Chris, apparently, who her father treated like a son. Oh, God, Mom and Dad were probably planning their wedding already. Dillon was getting married. Her turn next, right?

"Jo?"

"Sorry," she said. "Got lost in thought."

"You had a rough day. It's okay. I'll just meet you at the wedding. I'll be the dork in the bright pink Oxford shirt."

"Don't forget to tie a red jacket around your waist."

"Right." He started down the porch steps, heading to his truck parked behind the cabin. She didn't want him to go but she didn't know what to say to him if he stayed.

"And you have to carry my polka-dot underwear in your pocket."

Chris pulled something out of his back pocket. A pair of her panties, which he spun on his finger as he walked to his truck. Joey laughed. How could she not laugh with her underwear twirling in the wind? Chris stuffed them back into his pocket, got in his truck and drove away. For the second time in ten minutes she listened to wheels on gravel, the sound receding into the distance.

But when Chris drove away it was different.

When Chris drove away, Joey cried.

13

"YOU LET HIM drive away?" Kira asked. "You just…let him go?"

"What was I supposed to do?" Joey demanded. "Shoot him?"

"Why would you shoot him?"

"Because he cheated on me? Or on his wife with me? Or something?"

"I wasn't talking about Ben. I was talking about Chris! Why the hell would you let that beautiful bearded boy of yours drive off? He fucked your brains out against a wall, told you he loved you, showed up when Ben was there but didn't start a fight with him and then he left and you let him go?"

Joey didn't answer at first. She leaned back on the tree stump behind her and sighed. In an hour and a half she'd have to hop in her car and drive to the wedding, and she hadn't even taken a shower yet, put on her costume yet, fixed her hair yet. Every attempt she'd made at pulling herself together and getting ready had failed. Finally, she'd given up, put on her boots and coat, and went for a walk to clear her head. Somehow she'd ended up at the edge of the lake. She sat in the shadows of a million Douglas fir trees on a fallen log. In the distance, Mount Hood's peak rose up white against the blue-gray marbled sky. It was lovely, unbearably lovely, and she was lonely. Unbearably lonely.

"I don't know what to do," Joey finally said.

"Oh, I don't know, maybe tell Chris you're crazy about him, too. You are, aren't you?"

"I am."

"So what's the problem?"

"I just got out of a relationship two weeks ago. Two. Weeks. Ago. That's not even a whole month. That's half a month. That's a fortnight."

"What's a fortnight?"

"Two weeks!"

"You dumped a cheater. You're not a grieving widow."

"A cheater I'll have to see at work."

"Quit the job."

"You're the one who told me not to do anything drastic for six whole months, Kira," Joey said, shouting the words because it felt so good to yell.

"So? You don't have to listen to me. And that was before Chris. Rules exist. So do exceptions to the rules."

"This is not helping."

"Tell me—what's stopping you from getting together with Chris?"

"We've had sex like twenty times in eight days. Nothing stopped me from getting together with Chris."

"You know what I mean. Is this idea that you can't quit your job for a guy the only thing keeping you from quitting your job for a guy?"

"Kira. I cannot quit my job for a guy. I cannot. I will not. It's not happening. I love working."

"I know you do. But you can do your work somewhere else, right? I mean, every company on earth has a marketing department."

"I repeat—I am not quitting my job for a guy, especially a guy I have only been seeing for a couple weeks. Do you hear how insane that sounds? What if your sister called you up and said, 'Hey, I met a guy a couple weeks ago and now I'm quitting my job and moving twenty-five hundred miles away'? What would you say to that? I can guess what you'd say to that."

"I know what I'd say to that. I know *exactly* what I'd say to that."

"Tell me, then. What would you say to your baby sister if she made that phone call?"

"I would say..." Kira paused and laughed. "I would say, 'Is he a good man? Does he love you? Do you love him? Does he treat you well? Is he kind to others? Can you take care of yourself if the relationship falls apart?' And if she answered, 'Yes, yes, yes, yes, yes and yes,' then I'd say, 'You're a grown-ass woman. If this is what you want, go for it.' So let me ask you...what are your answers to those questions?"

"Kira."

"Joey."

Joey leaned forward and buried her head against her arms.

"I was so proud of myself," she said. "I graduated high school and I moved to Hawaii for college."

"It's a big move. You should be proud of yourself for that."

"Mom and Dad did nothing but worry about Dillon. That's all they did when we were in high school—worry about my brother. And I don't blame them. Kids tried to beat the shit out of him once a week his senior year. But I needed to get away from that. Age eighteen and I moved to an island in the center of the ocean."

"Good for you, Miss Independent."

"I got my own job, my own apartment. My family hasn't even had to help me move since I live so far away. And now if I move back? I'll be working for Dillon. And Mom and Dad are less than three hours away."

"You like them, right?"

"I love them."

"So the single only reason you don't want to quit your job and move back home is because you've somehow convinced yourself you shouldn't do that? Am I getting this right?"

"One week. I've been with Chris for only…one…week."

"That's not true."

"Fine. It was actually ten days."

"That's not what I mean. You knew him in high school, right?"

"Right…"

"For how long?"

"Since I was twelve. But," Joey said before Kira could counterattack, "I didn't know him for most of those years. He and Dillon lost touch for a few years after high school. They only started hanging out again after Dillon hired him to do some work earlier this year. He could be a serial killer, you know. Did you think about that? He's got the tools for it. And tarps. He keeps tarps with him in his truck."

"Because he's a contractor."

"Or a serial killer."

"You're scared shitless, aren't you?"

"God, yes."

Kira's laugh warmed Joey all the way from LA. Today was her birthday. Happy birthday to her. Heartache and impossible choices for her birthday. Just what she wanted.

"Are you scared shitless because you think you're in love with Chris? Or do you actually think you've been sleeping with a serial killer?"

"He's to die for in bed. But no, I don't think he's a serial killer."

"So you do think you're in love with Chris?"

"No."

"You don't think you're in love with Chris?"

"No."

"Joey."

"I don't know!" Joey's voice echoed off the lake, the mountain and through the trees. "Wow. That was loud."

"You feel better now that you've spooked all the wildlife in a fifty-mile radius?"

"Yes, actually."

"Good."

"Kira, tell me what to do."

"You know I can't do that. And you know you don't want me to. You're one of the smartest people I've ever met. Why is this so hard for you?"

"I dated a married guy for two years without realizing it. Do you know how stupid that makes me feel? I don't know if I can trust my own instincts anymore. It's like going through life thinking you're a good driver, a safe driver, and bam—you blink and cause a horrible car accident. Would you want to get behind the wheel again? Or would you be terrified?"

"Joey, you didn't cause a car accident. The only person who got hurt here was you. Ben caused the accident. You were just a passenger in his car of lies."

"His car of lies."

"His car of lies. Yes."

"I love you," Joey said.

"I know you do. And you know why? Because I'm awesome."

"True."

"I'm awesome. You know I'm awesome. And you love me because I'm awesome. So clearly your instincts about people aren't as shot as you think they are."

"You're not asking me to quit my job and move back to Oregon."

"I thought you liked Oregon."

"I love Oregon."

"So let me make sure I have this straight. Your pretty bearded boy with the good job, the magnificent cock and the ability to remodel an entire house singlehanded told you he loved you and asked you to maybe possibly consider living somewhere you love close to your family who you love while doing a job you'd love. Yes?"

"Well…yes."

"What a bastard."

"He's awful. I hate him."

"I can tell."

Joey sighed the sigh of sighs. She sighed so hard it almost surprised her she didn't capsize the canoes gliding across Lost Lake.

"I just want to do the right thing," Joey said. "I don't want to do the wrong thing again. Dating Ben was the wrong thing, and it was the wrong thing for two years of my life."

"Here's the problem. You're looking at this choice

likes it's right versus wrong. It's not right versus wrong. It's right versus left. You're at a crossroads. You can go left or right. Left to Hawaii and your current job. Right to Oregon, a new job and Chris. Both are good options. That's why it's so hard to decide. If this were a choice between right and wrong, it would be easy. But since both choices are good ones…"

"Since both choices are good ones, I'm sitting on a tree stump by a lake when I should be getting ready for my brother's wedding."

"You don't have to decide right now. It's not like it's do or die. Go to the wedding. Have fun. Go home to Hawaii tomorrow. Decide on your own time. If Chris really loves you, he'll give you time, right?"

"He'll give me time."

"Then stop stressing. Have fun tonight. Drink an extra glass of red wine for me, okay?"

"Done."

"I love you, JoJo."

"Love you, too, KiKi."

"Call me if you need me. But I have a date tonight so try not to need me until tomorrow morning after ten."

"Oh, thank God. Please distract me for the next half hour with your personal life. I'm so sick of mine."

"Can't. You have a wedding go to, and I have stuff to shave."

"Have fun."

"You, too."

Joey ended the call and stood up. She needed to hurry but she took one more look around, one more deep breath. In the fading light of sunset, the entire world seemed made up of shadows and shade. Only the highest trees on the highest part of the mountain

still shimmered in the golden light of day. Black water.
Green mountain. Blue sky. Brown earth. Red sun. She
wanted to stand here and take in all the beauty until
she had nothing but beauty within her. She wanted the
beauty to crowd out the confusion, the uncertainty and
the fear she carried around inside her head. And the
embarrassment, too. Kira was right. It wasn't her fault
Ben had lied to her. But knowing that in her mind and
knowing it in her heart were two different things. She
didn't feel ready to jump back into a relationship so
soon. It wasn't the relationship that scared her so much
as the jumping. This wasn't jumping off a diving board
into a pool. It felt like jumping out of an airplane into
the ocean.

Was it the ocean, though? Or did it just seem like
that? Maybe it only looked like the ocean from a distance but once she jumped in it she'd find herself in a
swimming pool. The deep end seemed very deep from
where she stood, however. The deep end meant quitting her job, moving twenty-five hundred miles away
from the place that had been her home her entire adult
life, dating a guy who was already in love with her, a
guy she'd only been seeing for a week—okay, ten days.
Ocean or swimming pool—a person could swim in both
or drown in both.

Yet…if she were honest with herself, a part of her
wanted to close her eyes and just cannonball. The past
two days since their fight in the cabin she had missed
Chris. She'd missed him more than she'd ever missed
Ben when he'd gone back to LA for work. Of course,
she'd known Ben would be back in a week or two and
Joey had no idea if or when she'd ever see Chris again
after she returned to Hawaii tomorrow. That possibility

felt…unacceptable. She had to see him again. Her entire body ached to see him again. Last night she lay alone in the bed he had crafted with his own hands and felt the absence of him inside her so keenly it hurt. Her entire body longed for him. Her hands missed his hands, her breasts missed his mouth and all of her missed his smile, his voice, his laugh in her ear and his cock inside her.

And him. Just him. She missed him. All of him. Every part of him. Even if he were standing next to her right now not touching her, not speaking, she would be happy.

But she couldn't stand here debating with herself a minute longer. She said her farewells to the lake and the mountain and headed down the path toward the cabin. As the sun set, the air chilled and she walked faster to stay warm. Yet when she passed the path leading to the stone cabin Chris had shown her two days ago, she slowed down. She saw a tendril of smoke escaping from the stone chimney. Was someone in the cabin? No one should be in the cabin, right? Lost Lake Village Rentals wasn't even open for business yet. Joey jogged down the walkway. Better to be late for the wedding than let one of Dillon's cabins burn down.

She reached the cabin and found all was well. It wasn't on fire, anyway. Someone had turned on all the lights in the cabin, however, and left the red door unlocked. She pushed the heavy wooden door open and found two men in the cabin moving furniture. One had a rocking chair in his hands that he placed by the fireplace. The other moved a wood frame sofa so that it lined up with the faded Persian rug on the floor.

"Ma'am?" One of the workmen saw her in the doorway. "You lost?"

"Oh, no," she said. "Sorry. My brother owns this cabin. I saw the smoke. I wanted to make sure the house wasn't burning down."

"Nothing burning down. Sorry to scare you," he said. "We're almost done here. Right?"

"Not yet," the other man said. "Couple more little things in the truck."

"I'll get them."

Joey looked around the cabin while the man got whatever it was out of his truck. All the furniture looked perfect for this cabin. Exactly what she would have chosen. She climbed the stairs to the loft and found a brass bed. It would need a new mattress and an old quilt. Quilts—not comforters or duvets. Real Amish quilts. On the bedside table was a metal lamp with a painted hand-blown glass shade. She'd seen similar lamps up at Timber Ridge Lodge. Downstairs she found a lawyer-style bookcase, antique walnut. Inside on the top shelf were a red leather dictionary, a black leather thesaurus, hardbound books on local flora and fauna and a blank book ready for ink on pages. The desk was also antique walnut, and with all the dings and nicks and chips in the wood, she would guess it had been around since the '50s or so. It must have weighed five hundred pounds from the looks of it. Now this was a desk someone could write their magnum opus on. Of course they'd need a...

"Excuse me, miss," the man said. Joey moved out of the way as the man sat a typewriter onto the top of the desk. A black Remington with black-and-white keys, a fresh black-and-red ribbon and polished to a high shine.

"Does it work?" she asked, staring at the vintage typewriter.

"It should," the man said. "Try it."

He handed her a blank invoice from his clipboard and Joey flipped it over to the back and rolled it through the typewriter. Instinctively she went to hit the on button before remembering it had no on button. Manual typewriter. She was the on button.

She put her fingers on the keys but didn't push them yet.

"I don't know what to write," she said. "I've never christened a typewriter before."

The man hung a plaque on a nail over the desk. "Just do what he says."

The sign—black text on white tin—simply read, *All you have to do is write one true sentence. —Ernest Hemingway.* That had been her idea, too, putting a few inspirational quotes in the cabin from artists and writers. Chris had listened to her ideas and implemented them in forty-eight hours. That said love to her more than his postsex declaration he'd made right over there by the wall. He'd listened to her, he valued her ideas, he made them come to life. And here was proof of it right at her fingertips. A manual typewriter. He'd picked out the one she would have picked out because it looked like the sort of typewriter one would use in a dream.

One true sentence, Hemingway said. Joey knew just what to write.

She put her fingers onto the keys, took a breath and slowly, carefully, typed out six words without a single typo.

I love you, too, Chris Steffensen.

14

CHRIS PULLED ON his pink Oxford, tied his red rain jacket around his waist and triple-checked that he did indeed have Joey's polka-dot bikini panties in his pocket. He did. Dillon and Oscar were holding their wedding at a waterfront reception venue on the Willamette River. They weren't bothering with a church wedding as neither of them went to church. No groomsmen or groomswomen, either. All guests were the wedding party. All the wedding party were guests. No dais. No altar. The wedding and the reception were one in the same. Dillon had told him he could even be late as the ceremony itself wouldn't start until about half an hour after the party started.

But Chris arrived a few minutes early in the hopes of finding Joey waiting for him. No such luck. No Joey. Not even a Jolene, although there was one very impressive-looking Dolly Parton walking around in a sequin dress and high heels, passing out glasses of champagne. Dillon and Oscar had gone all out on the '80s thing. Tears for Fears currently played in the background and a sign over the door read Enchantment Under the Sea. *Back to the Future* reference, right? Long time since he'd seen that movie. A Boy George look-alike handed him a wedding program. It was neon green and on the front it read, *Dillon and Oscar—Two of the '80s Greatest Hits*. According to the wedding program, Oscar had been born in 1980 and Dillon had been born in 1986 ergo they wanted their wedding celebration to also celebrate the decade of their births. Also they'd take any excuse to play the *Purple Rain* soundtrack and force their friends to feather their hair.

It was by far the most Portland wedding Chris had ever seen in his life. It could only be more Portland if the wedding were held in Voodoo Doughnuts with Elvis officiating.

But where the hell was Joey? He looked all over for her. She wasn't in the time machine telephone booth with Bill and Ted. He didn't find her in or by the mini Rocky boxing ring. She wasn't hanging out with The Outsiders who were, in fact, inside. She might have been standing behind the Poison cover band but he couldn't see past their hair.

He turned around ready to make another circuit of the room when Dillon came up to him.

"Happy wedding day, dude," Chris said, giving Dillon a hug.

"Looking good, man," Dillon said when he let Chris go. "Farmer Ted, right?"

"Joey's playing Sam but she's not here yet. Maybe she had trouble finding an ugly bridesmaid's dress." Chris looked Dillon up and down. Then he looked Oscar up and down across the room. "You're kidding, right?"

"Come on, you know they were secretly in love with each other," Dillon said.

Dillon wore gray pants, a white T-shirt, a leopard print vest and a leather jacket. Oscar wore a number nine Gordie Howe Detroit Red Wings jersey. Chris recognized the costumes immediately.

"Ferris Bueller and Cameron?"

"Ferris offered to take the blame for wrecking Cameron's dad's car, man. That's love. That's *true* love."

"What about the girlfriend? Sloan Whatever?"

"My theory is that Ferris was probably bi," Dillon said. "I'm not, but I think he was. Or she was his beard. Possible, right?"

"You've given this a little too much thought."

"No, I have given it *way* too much thought. Anyway, better go get my future husband away from my future mother-in-law so we can get this wedding thing started."

"Don't start yet. Joey's not here."

"She's not? She didn't come with you?"

"She wanted to meet me here."

Dillon narrowed his eyes at him. "Trouble in paradise?"

"I told her I was in love with her. It didn't go over well." Chris winced.

"You told her you loved her like a week after her breakup with that Ben guy? That Ben guy she was with for two years?"

"It was more like eight days. Bad idea?"

"Just ballsy, man. Very ballsy. Look, I love my sister with all my heart, and she's the greatest woman alive. But she's on the rebound now. She got her heart smashed up pretty bad and her pride. Might take her more than a couple weeks to get over that, you know?"

"I know. I do know. Just wishful thinking, I guess."

"Give her time. She's smart and you're the second best guy I know. She'll come around eventually." Dillon squeezed the back of Chris's shoulder. "Now, excuse me. I need to go marry the first best guy I know, and if my sister misses it, her loss. I'm not waiting another second."

Dillon walked away, and despite his dark mood, Chris couldn't help but smile. He remembered too many nights in high school when Dillon confessed his fears that not only would he never find anyone to love or anyone to love him, but that he might not even survive to adulthood to even give love a shot. And here he was, getting married. Legally married surrounded by friends and family and nothing but love. It gave Chris hope and he could use a little hope tonight. Joey left tomorrow. Hope was all he had.

Chris needed a drink. He walked past two John McClanes in bloody T-shirts and gray slacks, one Kevin Arnold from *The Wonder Years* in a vintage Jets jacket, the entire cast of *The Facts of Life* as played by guys in drag—Tutti even had her roller skates on—and four women dressed as *The Golden Girls*. They were probably coworkers of Oscar's. Dillon and Joey's pretty, young-looking mom was dressed as Andy from *The Goonies*. Their dad had on plaid pants and a Hawaiian shirt—not a good look for anyone but a spot-on Chunk costume. One woman walked passed him wearing a suit with shoulder pads so massive they almost reached her ears. She either had to be the blonde lady from *Night Court* or Cagney and/or Lacey. He couldn't recognize all the other costumes except maybe a Ghostbuster by the wedding cake and Baby from *Dirty Dancing*. Oddly enough Baby was in the corner. Seemingly by choice. Someone must have put her there.

Just then President Ronald Reagan—or a reasonable facsimile—tapped a fork on a champagne flute. The room fell silent.

"Mr. Gorbachev," Reagan said in a very good Reagan voice, "marry these two men."

A man in a fake bald wig with a painted-on forehead birthmark and a gray suit stepped into the center of the floor.

Ferris/Dillon and Cameron/Oscar stepped into the center of the circle created by the guests. They were smiling so broadly it made Chris's cheeks ache just looking at them. He wanted this for himself. Maybe not a wedding where half the guests were dressed as members of the A-Team but he wanted this—his friends everywhere, his parents, Joey's parents and a life together with her. Four days ago he'd strained a muscle in his shoulder while climbing a cottonwood to cut down some dead and overhanging branches. When Joey caught him taking ibuprofen, she'd put him on the bed and rubbed his shoulders and back for two hours.

Two hours.

It hadn't even been foreplay, although they did have sex later than night. Joey had felt that he was hurt and she'd spent two hours trying to make him feel better. How could he not fall in love with a woman who was that sweet? And she gave damn good backrubs, too. God, he missed her.

With an instrumental version of "Time After Time" playing softly in the background, Dillon and Oscar exchanged their vows. Out of the corner of his eye he saw Angela and Tony from *Who's the Boss?* wiping tears off their cheeks. And when the couple kissed, "The Final Countdown" by Europe began to play. It was all strangely moving. And movingly strange. And mostly just strange. Everyone clapped at the kiss, even Chris, who still wasn't sold on Dillon's theory that Ferris and Cameron had been secretly in love with each other. Although if they had been, that would have made for one hell of a sequel.

With the ceremony over, Dolly Parton once again walked the room distributing drinks. Chris grabbed a glass of champagne and turned around, intending to head for the deck.

And standing by the door to the club was a girl dressed in a green sweater vest and jeans.

A green sweater vest and jeans.

A green sweater vest...

Wait.

The girl raised her hand and waved at him. Chris laughed. He laughed so hard it hurt.

Joey shook her head and walked over to him.

"You're messing up the scene, you know," she said, reaching out and grabbing on to the lapels of his pink Oxford shirt. "You're supposed to say your line."

"If you remember correctly, when we watched the movie last week, we didn't get to the end because someone started chewing on my earlobe and we know where that always ends. You have to remind me—what's my line?"

"After the wedding, Sam sees Jake Ryan standing outside his car waiting for her and she points at herself and mouths, 'Me?' And Jake whispers back, 'Yeah, you.'"

"But if I remember right, doesn't Jake come and get Sam after the wedding? Not Farmer Ted?"

"We're starring in the sexy gender swap remake of *Sixteen Candles* called *Twenty-Six Candles*, where Joey Ryan tells Farmer Chris she's sorry for flipping out when Farmer Chris said he loved her."

"This is a much better version of the movie."

"I hope so," she said. "I hope I'm not screwing everything up here. But I—"

"What? Tell me," Chris said.

When Joey took his hand in hers, Chris's heart balled up in his chest like a fist and hit the inside of his rib cage. Talk about good pain.

"I saw the cabin you fixed up like I said you should. The desk and the typewriter and everything."

"You like it?"

"Love it," she said. "I tested the typewriter. See?" She dug in her pocket for a piece of paper and passed it to him.

"Joey, this is an invoice from Northwest Vintage Furniture. I'm touched."

"Flip it over."

Chris stared at the words, the beautiful words in black on white.

"Joey…" He looked up at her, his heart in his throat, his throat in his feet.

"I kept thinking about what I *should* do instead of about what I wanted to do and what I *should* feel instead of what I did feel. Obviously you shouldn't start dating again two weeks after a bad breakup. And obviously you shouldn't fall in love with the guy you were seeing on the rebound. But obviously I did."

"I'm…" Chris shook his head. "I'm speechless."

"Then find a better use for your mouth than talking."

He took her face in his hands and looked into her eyes. Joey, his Joey, the same Joey he'd loved when he was eighteen and loved now at twenty-eight and would love when he was eighty-eight, ninety-eight, a hundred and eight. He pressed his lips to hers and held her close, her body falling against his, soft and warm and all his. All his now, and if he were the luckiest man on earth, all his forever.

Joey pulled away, laughing and grinning.

"What?" Chris asked.

"My cousin Lionel Ritchie just gave us a dirty look. We are kind of making out in the middle of someone else's wedding."

Chris waved at him and mouthed, "Hello." A man walked passed them, a very familiar-looking man.

"Is that guy dressed as Ron Jeremy?" Joey whispered in his ear.

"No," Chris replied. "That's actually Ron Jeremy."

"Portland," Joey said.

Joey grabbed Chris's hand and he let her drag him over to Oscar and Dillon. She threw herself into Dillon's arms and hugged him hard.

"That was the best wedding ever," she said.

"Yes, I know. Why are you wearing my sweater vest?" Dillon asked, looking her up and down.

"I stole it to seduce Chris. It worked."

"Damn," Dillon said. "Sweater vest kink? You are a deviant, aren't you?" he said to Chris. Chris shrugged but didn't deny it.

"Consider it a birthday present to me that I stole from you since you stole my birthday from me," Joey said, poking him in the chest.

"Oh, shit, it is your birthday," Dillon said. "Totally forgot. You know, because of my wedding. I'm married, by the way. Have you met my husband?"

"She has," Oscar said. "Also, your brother is a liar. We didn't forget your birthday at all. We simply borrowed it. Now you can have it back. Present?"

"Present," Dillon said. "Chris? Are we doing this present thing?"

"We're doing it." Chris reached into his pants pocket and pulled out a key ring with ten keys on it.

Joey looked at him and at Dillon and at Oscar and back at him.

"What's going on?" she asked.

"Your real birthday present," Dillon said. "Not a sweater vest. Pick one."

"Pick one what?" she asked.

"These are the ten keys for the ten cabins of Lost Lake Village Rentals. One is yours."

JOEY'S MOUTH FELL open for a second; she was dumbfounded. She wasn't sure she'd ever been dumbfounded before. Shocked. Stunned. Flabbergasted, yes. But never dumbfounded.

"You're giving me a cabin?" she asked. "But I haven't even said I'd take the job yet."

"You should take it," Dillon said, grinning. "But it's not about the job. First, sorry about stealing your birthday to use for our wedding. And second, I just want you to come home more often. I miss you. We all miss you. And no pressure. We'll sign the cabin over to you and you'll be the sole owner. When you're in Hawaii, we can rent it out as part of Lost Lake Village Rentals, or you can lock it up and Chris will check it every couple of days to make sure the pipes don't freeze or whatever happens out there in nature. You get a cabin to own and stay in as often or a seldom as you want. Chris fixed up eight of them and he's got two more to do by spring. But you can pick any one of them."

Chris could see Joey's shaking hand when she reached for the key chain.

"I want the one we grew up in," she said. "Our cabin. Mom and Dad gave it to you so we'll keep it in the family. Our family." She looked at Chris when she said it because when she said "our" she meant the one she and Chris had shared all week, made love in all week, ate breakfast together in all week. "Our cabin" meant hers and Chris's.

"All yours," Chris said, and gave her the key.

"Happy birthday, Jo," Dillon said.

"Yes," she said.

"That wasn't a yes or no question," Dillon said. "It wasn't even a question at all."

"Yes, I'll take the job," she said. "Chris talked me into it."

"I did?" he asked.

"Okay, you didn't talk me into it but the artist's retreat cabin did. Seeing my ideas turned into reality in forty-eight hours? You got me. This could be my dream job."

"You start tomorrow," Dillon said. "But don't call your bosses for a week or more. We'll be on our honeymoon. Starting now." Dillon kissed Oscar so passionately and dramatically Joey could only roll her eyes.

"You want to get out of here?" Chris asked in her ear.

"Leave my brother's wedding reception?"

Chris glanced over at Oscar and Dillon, who were still making out, and then back at her.

"There's a back room here," she said. "The door has a lock on it."

"Can you still hear the music in the room?" Chris asked.

"Yeah. So?"

"I can't get a boner to 'The Safety Dance.' Let's go outside."

Chris grabbed her by the hand and led her past three Jellicle cats, one Seagull minus the Flock and a very tall but adorable Mary Lou Retton in her American flag leotard.

"Where are we going?" she asked.

"Back to the future," he said.

Hand in hand they left the reception and weaved through the lines of parked cars until they reached Chris's truck. He opened the door for her, she got inside and he followed, shutting the door with a decisive slam. He put his keys in the ignition and turned on the radio. "Interstate Love Song" by the Stone Temple Pilots was playing.

"I feel so much better now." He sighed and leaned his head back against the seat with his eyes closed.

"It is a good song."

"No, I feel better because you're here." He turned his head and looked at her.

"I'm here. And I'm going to stay here."

"No more Hawaii?"

"I'll go back tomorrow and put in my two weeks' notice. And I'll start packing up."

"You don't have to. I'll still love you from here even if you're there."

"I know I don't have to," she said, "but I want to."

"What else do you want to do?" he asked with a grin. He had the best smile of any man she'd ever known. When not smiling he looked serious and somber, but when he grinned, it was impossible not to grin back.

"I want to come home. I want to see my family more often. I want to make Lost Lake Village amazing. But more than anything, I want to do this." She wrapped her arms around his shoulders and pulled him to her. He kissed her as he lowered her onto her back on the leather bench seat of the truck. She didn't waste any time getting her hands between them, unbuttoning his jeans and stroking him. He was rock hard in her hand. She ached to have him inside her.

"We're in public, sort of." He didn't seem to mind that too much as he'd already pushed her vest and shirt up to her neck and unhooked her bra.

"I don't care. I need you," she said as he unzipped her jeans and yanked them down her thighs. "I've needed you for three days."

Chris slipped his fingers into her and inhaled sharply. "You do need me, don't you?" he asked. "You're so fucking wet."

"For you. All for you." She started to run her hands through his hair and found that she couldn't. "Chris? What the hell is in your hair? It's…"

"What?"

"It's crunchy."

"Mousse," Chris said. "It's supposed to be the '80s, right?"

"Okay, fuck me fast because when we're done, I'm washing your hair in the river if I have to. And if that doesn't work, I'm getting a razor."

"I didn't hear anything after you said 'fuck me fast.'"

"That was the important part."

Chris laughed and kissed her again. Braced between her knees, he rolled on the condom and sunk down on top of her. This was no time for niceties, no time for whispering sweet nothings or making plans for the future. They could do all that later. Now they just needed to fuck each other, hard and without further delay. Chris thrust deep into her and Joey groaned as quietly as she could. That was it, that was what she needed. The aching inside her was so sharp and so sweet and his cock was the cause and the cure of it. Joey held tight to him, as tight as she could as she rocked her hips into his again and again, dizzy from the pleasure, racked with need. Her inner muscles contracted and clenched around him as he pumped into her with rough and hungry thrusts. On the narrow truck seat, they could barely move, which only made it all hotter and sexier and more desperate. Her orgasm hit her hard, all at once with barely any warning. She flinched and gasped as her vagina spasmed around Chris. He knelt over her and took her naked breasts into his large hands. With long rough thrusts he rode her to the beautiful end, coming in silence and then sinking onto her again. He kissed her face, her lips, her neck and nipples.

"This has been a good day," she said. She drew a heart in the fog on the window.

"Happy birthday," Chris said.

"Very happy. And Happy Halloween," she said, wrapping her arms around his shoulders. He was still hard, still inside her. Maybe they'd make love one more time before going back to the reception. Maybe they wouldn't go back at all.

"Oh, yeah, it's Halloween, too, isn't it?" he asked. "Trick or treat?"

"Trick."

"I totally tricked you into falling in love with me so you'd stay," Chris said. "And it worked."

"That wasn't a trick," Joey said.

"It wasn't? What was it then?"

She kissed him and then kissed him again and then one more time for good measure.

"My treat."

* * * * *

Want more sexy stories set on Mount Hood, Oregon?
There are two more books in Tiffany Reisz's
MEN AT WORK *miniseries,*
HER NAUGHTY HOLIDAY
and ONE HOT DECEMBER,
coming November and December 2016,
only from Harlequin Blaze!

REQUEST YOUR FREE BOOKS!
2 FREE NOVELS PLUS 2 FREE GIFTS!

Ⓗ HARLEQUIN®

Blaze

red-hot reads!

HB15

"I'm not going to try to convince you to do something you don't want to do," Clover said.

"Why not?"

"Because no means no."

"I didn't say no. Come on. I'm a businessman. Let's haggle."

Clover laughed a nervous laugh, almost a giggle. She sat behind her desk and Erick sat on the desk next to her.

"You're pretty when you laugh," he said. "But you're also pretty when you don't laugh."

"You're sweet," she said. "I feel like I shouldn't have brought this up."

"So do you really need someone to play boyfriend for the week? It's that bad with your family?"

She sighed heavily and sat back.

"It's hard," she said. "They love me but that doesn't make the stuff they say easier to hear. They think they're saying 'We love you and we want you to be happy,' but what I hear is 'You're inadequate, you're a disappointment and you haven't done what you're supposed to do to make *us* happy.'"

He grinned at her and shrugged. "You think I'm cute?" he asked.

"You're hot," she said. "Like UPS-driver hot."

"That's hot."

"Smoking."

"This is fun," he said. "Why haven't we ever flirted with each other before?"

"You know, my parents would probably be very impressed if they thought I were dating a single father. They'd think that was a ready-made family."

"You really want me to be your boyfriend?" Erick asked. He already planned on doing it. He'd do anything for this woman, including but not limited to pretending to be her boyfriend for a couple days.

"I would appreciate it," she said.

"We can have sex all week, too, right?"

"Okay."

"What?" Erick burst into laughter.

"What?" she repeated. "Why are you laughing?"

"I didn't think you'd say yes. I was joking."

"You were?" Her blue eyes went wide.

"Well…yeah. I mean, not that I don't want to. I do want to. I swear to God, I thought you'd say no. I never guessed you'd say yes, not in a million years."

"And why not?"

Don't miss HER NAUGHTY HOLIDAY
by Tiffany Reisz, available November 2016 wherever
Harlequin® Blaze® books and ebooks are sold.

www.Harlequin.com

HBEXP1016

Reading Has Its Rewards

Earn **FREE BOOKS!**

Register at **Harlequin My Rewards** and submit your Harlequin purchases from wherever you shop to earn points for free books and other exclusive rewards.

Plus submit your purchases from now till May 30th for a chance to win a $500 Visa Card*.

Visit **HarlequinMyRewards.com** today

Earn **FREE** REWARDS
Join Today!
HarlequinMyRewards.com

MYR16R1